DEATH OF A DENTIST

Previous mysteries by M. C. Beaton

Hamish Macbeth

Death of a Macho Man
Death of a Nag
Death of a Charming Man
Death of a Gossip
Death of a Cad
Death of an Outsider
Death of a Perfect Wife
Death of a Hussy
Death of a Snob
Death of a Prankster
Death of a Glutton
Death of a Travelling Man

Agatha Raisin

Agatha Raisin and the Quiche of Death
Agatha Raisin and the Vicious Vet

M.C. BEATON

DEATH OF A DENTIST

THE MYSTERIOUS PRESS

Published by Warner Books

A Time Warner Company

Mysterious Press books are published by Warner Books, Inc., 1271 Avenue of the Americas, New York, NY 10020.

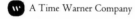 A Time Warner Company

The Mysterious Press name and logo are registered trademarks of Warner Books, Inc.
Printed in the United States of America
First Printing: August 1997

10 9 8 7 6 5 4 3 2 1

Library of Congress Cataloging-in-Publication Data

Beaton, M. C.
    Death of a dentist / M.C. Beaton.
        p.   cm.
    ISBN 0–89296–643–2
    I. Macbeth, Hamish (Fictitious character)—Fiction.   2. Dentist—
Scotland—Highlands—Fiction.   3. Highlands (Scotland)—Fiction.
I. Title.
PR6052.E196D382   1997
823'.914—dc20
                                                    96-42016
                                                    CIP

For Jane Sybilla Crosland
with love

CHAPTER ONE

For there was never yet a philosopher,
That could endure the toothache patiently.

—William Shakespeare

It was a chill autumn in the Highlands of Scotland when Police Constable Hamish Macbeth awoke in hell.

The whole side of his jaw was a burning mass of pain.

Toothache. The sort of toothache so bad you cannot tell which tooth is infected because the pain runs through them all.

His dentist was in Inverness and he felt he could not bear the long drive. Lochdubh, the village in which his police station was situated, did not boast a dentist. The nearest one was at Braikie, a small town twenty miles away. The dentist there was Frederick Gilchrist.

The problem was that Hamish Macbeth still had all his teeth and meant to keep them all and Mr. Gilchrist had a reputation for pulling out teeth rather than saving them, which suited the locals, who still preferred to have their teeth drawn and a "nice" set of dentures put in. Also Gilchrist, in these days of high dental charges, was cheap.

One summer visitor complained bitterly that Gilchrist had performed The Great Australian Trench on her. Australian dentists had gained the unfair reputation for casually letting the drill slide across as many teeth as possible, therefore getting themselves a lucrative and steady customer. And although Mr. Gilchrist was Scottish, he was reputed to have performed this piece of supposedly Australian malpractice. Mrs. Harrison, a local widow, alleged nastily that she had been sexually molested by Gilchrist while unconscious under gas, but Mrs. Harrison was a strange woman who always seemed to think every man was lusting after her and so her charge was not taken very seriously, and as she had not reported it to the police, but only to everyone else who would listen, there had been no excuse for Hamish Macbeth to take the matter further.

And yet the pain was so fierce that by the time he had dressed, he had argued himself into sacrificing one tooth.

He dialled Gilchrist's number. Gilchrist's receptionist, Maggie Bane, answered the telephone and to Hamish's frantic appeal for help said sourly he would just need to come along and take his chances. Mr. Gilchrist was very busy. Come at three and maybe he'll fit you in.

Hamish then went to the bathroom and scrabbled in the kitchen cabinet, looking for aspirin and found none. He petulantly slammed the cabinet door shut. It fell off the wall into the handbasin, and cracked the porcelain of the handbasin before sending large shards of glass from its shattered glass doors onto the bathroom floor.

He looked at his watch through a red mist of pain. Eight o'clock in the morning. Dear God, he wouldn't *live* until the afternoon. A sorry, lanky figure in his worn police uniform, he left the police station and made his way rapidly along the waterfront to Dr. Brodie's home.

Angela, the doctor's wife, answered the door in her dressing gown. "Why, Hamish, you're early," she cried.

"I need help," moaned Hamish. "I'm dying."

"Come in. He's in the kitchen."

Dr. Brodie, wrapped in a camel hair dressing gown, looked up as Hamish entered, a piece of toast and marmalade halfway to his lips. "Hamish!" he said. "You look like death."

"You've got to give me something quick," gabbled Hamish, grabbing his arm. "I am in the mortal pain. I haff the toothache."

"You look as if you've got mad cow disease," said Dr. Brodie sourly, jerking his arm away. "Oh, very well, Hamish. Sit yourself down while I get my bag."

Hamish sank down in a chair and clutched his jaw. One of Angela's cats leapt lightly on the table, studied Hamish with curious eyes and then began to drink the milk out of the jug.

Dr. Brodie came back with his bag, opened it, and took out a small torch. "Now, open wide Hamish. Which one is it?"

"It feels like all of them," said Hamish. He opened his mouth and pointed to the lower left of his jaw.

Dr. Brodie shone the torch in his mouth. "Ah, yes, nasty."

"Nasty what?" demanded Hamish.

"You've got an abscess there. The bottom right-hand molar. Ugh! I don't know that a dentist could treat you until it's cleared up. I'll give you a shot of antibiotic. I'll need to go to the surgery. Stay here and Angela'll get you a coffee. I'll need to get dressed."

"Where am I getting this injection?"

"In the backside."

"Then I will be coming with you."

"Why?"

Hamish blushed. "I do not want your wife seeing my bare bum."

Dr. Brodie laughed. "I'm glad there's one woman left in this village you don't want to show your bum to."

When he had gone upstairs to change, Hamish whimpered, "No coffee, Angela. I'm in such awfy pain, I couldnae get it past my lips."

"You're nothing but a big baby, Hamish Macbeth," said Angela, her thin face lighting up with amusement.

"Women!" said Hamish sourly. "All that talk about maternal feelings and womanly sympathy is chust the myth."

"If the abscess is that bad, why did you let it go so far?"

"I felt a few twinges," muttered Hamish, "but, och, I thought I had the cold in the face."

Angela smiled again at him, sat down at the coffee table, grabbed the cat by the scruff of the neck and dragged its face out of the milk jug, poured some in her coffee, and picked up a book, saying before she started to read, "I am sure you do not feel like talking."

Hamish glared at her and nursed his jaw. Dr. Brodie eventually appeared. "Let's get to the surgery, Hamish, and spare your blushes."

They walked silently along the waterfront. The day was cold and still. Smoke from the cottage chimneys rose straight up into the clear air. A heron sailed lazily over the sea loch. The village of Lochdubh in Sutherland—that county which is as far north in mainland Britain as you can go—dreamed in the pale sunlight making one sad constable feel like a noisy riot of pain.

Once in the surgery, Dr. Brodie injected Hamish with a stiff shot of antibiotics, gave him a prescription for antibiotic pills and told him to go home and lie down. Hamish had told him about the appointment with Gilchrist. "You'd best cancel it," said Dr. Brodie, "until that abscess has cleared up. You don't want to go to Gilchrist anyway. He'll pull the tooth and there's no need for that these days. You'd be better off in Inverness. There's been some awfully nasty stories about Gilchrist circling about."

Hamish crept off back to the police station. He had bought a bottle of aspirin from Patel's, the local supermarket on the road there. He took three aspirin, swallowing them down with a stiff glass of whisky. He undressed slowly and climbed back into bed, willing the pain to go away. To take his mind off the pain, he began to think of Gilchrist and all the rumours about the man, and then he suddenly fell asleep.

He awoke two hours later. The pain had almost gone, but he was frightened to get out of bed in case that dreadful pain came roaring back. He clasped his hands behind his head and stared at the ceiling. He missed his dog, Towser, who had died so suddenly. Towser would have lain on the end of the bed and wagged his tail and he, Hamish, would have felt that someone in the whole wide world cared about his suffering. Priscilla Halburton-Smythe, the once love of his life, had gone to London to stay with friends and no other woman had come along to fill the gap left by her going. They had once been unofficially engaged, but he had broken off the relationship because of Priscilla's odd coldness when he had tried to make love to her. He missed her, but he tried to tell himself that missing Priscilla had simply become a habit.

His thoughts then turned to Gilchrist and his Highland curiosity about the dentist was fully roused. Hamish had never met the man. He would phone up and say he could not see him that day and then he would make another appointment. If Gilchrist showed any signs of removing the tooth, he would remove himself from that dentist's chair and go to Inverness. But that way he would be able to see the dentist and form his own opinion. It was all so easy to lose one's reputation in the Highlands of Scotland where one tall tale was embellished and passed around and another added to it.

The phone rang shrilly from the police station office. He got gingerly out of bed and went to answer it. It was from the owner of a hotel fifteen miles away on the Lairg road, complaining he had been burgled the night before.

Hamish promised to be over as soon as he could, dressed again, got into the police Land Rover and drove out to The Scotsman Hotel where the burglary had taken place. He expected to find vandalism, broken windows, the bar a mess, but it transpired that the break-in had been a professional one. The safe in the office had been broken into and the week's takings stolen.

The safe looked heavy and massive and the door undamaged.

"How did they get into that?" he asked, pushing back his peaked cap and scratching his fiery red hair.

The manager, Brian Macbean, nodded to two men, who swung the safe round.

"Oh, my," said Hamish. For the back of the safe had been made of a panel of chipboard which the burglar had simply sawn through.

He took out his notebook. "Can we sit down, Mr. Macbean, and I'll take some notes. Then I'll phone Strathbane and get them to send a forensic team over. How much was in the safe?"

"Two hundred and fifty thousand pounds."

"What on earth were you doing keeping that amount of money on the premises?"

"It's the giant prize for this Saturday night's bingo session. Man, we've got folk coming from every part of the Highlands."

"So someone knew about it, and someone knew about the back of the safe."

Macbean, a squat, burly man with thinning hair, looked morose. "The big bingo night's been in all the local papers, so it has."

"But why cash?" Hamish was puzzled. "A cheque would ha' done."

"That was the attraction. It was all in twenty pound notes. All the press photographers were coming. It would have made the grand picture, some winner with all those notes."

Hamish licked the end of his pencil. "So why the wooden back on the safe?"

"I needed a safe and there was this one over at the auction rooms in Inverness. I thought that would do me fine."

"And probably charged the owners for a real safe."

Macbean looked mulishly at the floor and did not reply.

Hamish patiently took him through exactly when the theft had been discovered and then said, "Who knew the safe had a wooden back?"

"The barman, Johnny King, and one of the waiters, Peter Sampson. They helped me bring it back from Inverness."

"What about your family?"

"Well, of course they knew. My wife, Agnes, and my girl, Darleen."

Hamish racked through his mind for any gossip he might have heard about Macbean's family, but could think of nothing in particular. "I'll need to interview the barman and the waiter," he said, "and then I'll talk to your wife and daughter."

"Whit! Leave my family out of it."

"Don't be daft, Mr. Macbean. They might have seen something or heard something. How old is Darleen?"

"Twenty-two."

"Where is she now?"

"She's over at the dentist in Braikie with her mother."

Gilchrist again, thought Hamish, and then realised with a sort of glad wonder that the hellish pain in his tooth had subsided.

"How come a Highland hotel can afford to offer such a huge money prize?"

"We run the bingo nights all year round with small prizes and the profits are put in the bank. I drew the big money out of the bank in the middle of the week."

"I'll just use the phone there," he said, "and call Strathbane, and then I'll take a look around."

Detective Chief Inspector Blair when contacted said he was busy on a drugs job but would send his sidekick, Jimmy Anderson, over with a forensic team.

Hamish examined the hotel office. Apart from the gaping hole in the back of the safe, there was no other sign of a break-in that he could see. "You discovered this in the morning," he said. "What was going on here last night?"

"There was a ceilidh."

"How many people?"

"About a hundred or so. But the office was locked."

Hamish examined the office door. It was wooden with a frosted-glass panel. The lock was a simple Yale one, easily picked.

The barman and the waiter were brought in. Hamish questioned them closely. They hadn't finished their duties until one in the morning and then had gone straight to bed. The barman, Johnny King, was a sinister-looking man in his thirties with his hair worn in a ponytail and his thin face marred by a long scar. Peter Sampson, the waiter, was a small, smooth-faced youth of about twenty.

After he had finished interviewing them, Hamish walked around the public rooms of the hotel. It was typical of the more depressing type of Highland hotel, everything in pine and plastic and with the once gaudy carpets looking as if they badly needed shampooing. Tartan curtains hung at the windows and the walls were ornamented with plastic claymores and plastic shields along with bad murals of depressing historical events like the Battle of Culloden and the Massacre of Glencoe. The artist had not liked Bonnie Prince Charlie, for there he was with a cowardly look on his white face fleeing the Battle of Culloden. And he hadn't liked the Campbells either, witness their savage and gleeful faces as they massacred the Macdonalds of Glencoe.

"What's the polis doing here?" demanded a shrill voice behind him.

He swung round. A small blonde middle-aged woman stood glaring at him. Her hair was wound around a forest of pink plastic rollers and a cigarette hung from thin lips, painted orange. Beside her stood a tall, sulky girl in micro skirt and black suede thigh boots, fringed suede jacket and purple blouse. Her makeup was dead-white, her lipstick purple and her black hair gelled into spikes.

"Mrs. Macbean?"

"Aye, what's it to you?"

"The safe in the office was broken into last night, Mrs. Macbean," explained Hamish patiently.

"The bingo money! It's gone?"

"All gone," said Hamish.

"Cool," said Darleen. Her eyes were flat and dead. Valium or sheer bovine stupidity, thought Hamish.

"Where is he?" demanded Mrs. Macbean.

"In the office," said Hamish, and then turned away as he heard cars driving up outside.

He went out to meet the contingent from Strathbane.

Detective Jimmy Anderson's foxy features lit up in a grin when he saw Hamish.

"If it isnae Mr. Death hisself," he said cheerfully. "Where's the body? Wi' the great Hamish Macbeth on the scene, there's bound to be a body."

"No body. The safe's been broken into like I told you. I figure someone from the hotel did it."

"Aye, maybe, Hamish. But what makes you think that?"

"I chust have this feeling."

"The seer of Lochdubh," jeered Jimmy. "Man, I could murder a dram. Any chance of them opening up that bar?"

"You shouldnae be thinking o' drinking on duty," said Hamish primly.

"Och, Hamish, it's only on the TV that they say things like that."

"And in police regulations."

"If you paid any attention to police regulations, you would smarten up that horrible uniform. Your trousers are so shiny I can see ma face in them."

"Are we going to investigate this," snapped Hamish, "or are we going to stand here all day trading insults?"

"Where's the body, then?" said Jimmy with a sigh.

"If you mean the safe, it's in the office. Afore you go in, Jimmy, is there any gossip about Macbean?"

"Not that I've heard. Somat Enterprises, a Glasgow company who owns this place, employed him two years ago. The food's rotten and the drinks are suspect, but they come for the bingo and the dancing. You know how it is, Hamish, it's not as if Sutherland is a swinging place. No competition. Oh, well, lead the way."

Macbean was standing outside the office in the entrance hall. Through the open office door, the white-coated forensic team were busy dusting everything for fingerprints.

"Damn," muttered Hamish. "Two of the men turned the safe around. Their fingerprints will be on it."

"I'll tell them," said Jimmy.

"You stupid fool," Mrs. Macbean suddenly shouted in her husband's face. One pink roller shaken loose by her rage fell onto the carpet. "I tellt ye that safe was silly. But you had tae go and dae things on the cheap."

"Shut your face," growled Macbean, "and go and do something to yourself. You look a right fright with them curlers in."

Hamish's tooth gave a sinister twinge. "Wait a bit, Mrs. Macbean," he said, "you went to the dentist in Braikie."

"Aye."

"What's Gilchrist like?"

She looked at him in amazement. "It wisnae me. It was Darleen that had the toothache."

Hamish turned questioningly to Darleen, who was slumped against the wall, studying her long purple fingernails.

"Darleen?"

She suddenly opened her mouth and pointed to the bottom front row of her teeth where there was a gap.

"He pulled your tooth?"

"Too right."

"Couldn't he have saved it?"

"Whit fur?"

"Because teeth can be saved these days."

Darleen stifled a yawn. "No shit, Sherlock."

"Whit the hell are you asking questions about some poxy dentist when you're supposed to be finding out who burgled my safe?" howled Macbean.

"I'm working on something else," said Hamish.

Jimmy Anderson came out of the office. "Okay, I'll take you one at a time. There's no need for you any mair, Hamish. You can get back to your sheep dip papers or whatever exciting things you usually do in Lochdubh."

Hamish went reluctantly. There was an odd smell of villainy about the hotel. "I'll type up my notes for you," he said stiffly to Jimmy.

"I wouldnae bother," said Jimmy cheerfully. "When does that bar open?"

Hamish left. He drove back to Lochdubh but instead of going to the station, he stopped at the Tommel Castle Hotel just outside the village. The hotel was owned by Colonel

Halburton-Smythe, Priscilla's father, a landowner who, on Hamish's suggestion, had turned his family home into a hotel when he was in danger of going bankrupt. The hotel had prospered, first through the efforts of Priscilla and then under the efficient management of Mr. Johnson, the manager. He went through to the hotel office where Mr. Johnson was rattling the keys of a computer. Hamish pulled up a chair to the desk and sat down opposite the manager. "Help yourself to coffee, Hamish," said the manager, jerking his head in the direction of a coffee machine in the corner.

Hamish rose and helped himself to a mugful of coffee and sat down again. "That's that," said Mr. Johnson with a sigh. "I miss Priscilla. She's a dab hand at the accounts. What brings you, Hamish, or are you just chasing a free cup of coffee?"

"There's been a burglary over at The Scotsman."

"Druggies from Inverness?"

"No, the safe was robbed. The bingo prize money. Two hundred and fifty thousand pounds."

"Did they blow it?"

"No, Macbean got the safe on the cheap at an auction in Inverness. It had a wooden back."

"I mind that safe. I was at that auction myself. That safe was made by a company nobody had ever heard of. I couldn't believe that wooden back."

"So what's the gossip about Macbean?"

"Sour man with a slag of a wife and a drip of a daughter. Came here about two years ago. Somat Enterprises seem to have given him a free hand. It's run by some Scottish Greek. Got lots of sleazy restaurants and dreary hotels. As far as I can gather, as long as The Scotsman showed a profit, he didn't interfere. Macbean may have been creaming some of the profits, but he'd need to be smarter than I think he is, because Somat has a team of ferocious auditors who regularly check the books.

Macbean thought up the bingo night and it's been a big success. Do you know the colonel even had the stupidity to suggest we do the same thing? People come here for the fishing
and shooting and the country house life, they don't want a lot
of peasants cluttering up the place."

"What about the staff?"

"Don't know. You know what it's like trying to get staff up
here, Hamish. No one's anxious to check out references too
closely."

"Well it's got nothing to do with me now." Hamish sipped
his coffee and winced as the hot liquid washed around his bad
tooth. "Jimmy Anderson's taken over. It'll be a long slog—
checking out Macbean's past, checking out the staff's past,
checking out Macbean's bankbook."

"It's more Blair's line to keep you off a case, Hamish."

"Aye, well, there been talk about Blair's liver being a wee bit
damaged and Jimmy Anderson aye goes through a personality
change when he sniffs promotion." He winced again.

"Toothache?"

"I've got an abscess. Dr. Brodie gave me a shot of antibiotic.
I was going over to see Gilchrist. Oh, I forgot to say I wouldn't
be going."

"I wouldn't go near that butcher, Hamish. There was a bit of
a scandal. Jock Mackay over at Braikie got a tooth pulled and
Gilchrist broke his jaw. Jock had impacted roots and the tooth
should have been sawn in half and then taken out a bit at a
time. Turned out Gilchrist hadn't even X-rayed him first. Folks
told him to sue, but you know what it's like. A lot of them are
brought up to think that doctors, lawyers and dentists are little
gods. They never seem to think that they're just like the butcher
or the baker. You get bad meat from the butcher, you find another butcher, but they'll stick with a bad doctor or a bad dentist until the end of time."

"Can I use your phone? I might go over myself tomorrow, now that I've got the excuse. What does Gilchrist look like?"

"White."

"I didn't think he was African or Indian."

"No, I mean, very white, big white face, big white hands like uncooked pork sausages, very pale eyes, thick white hair, white eyebrows, white coat like the ones the American dentists wear."

"Age?"

"Fifties, at a guess. Bit of a ladies' man, by all accounts. Use the phone by all means, but only ask for a checkup or that man will have the pliers out and all your teeth out."

Hamish dialled the dentist's number. Maggie Bane answered the phone. He had never met her any more than he had ever met the dentist although he knew her name and had heard of her. Her voice on the phone was sharp and peremptory and he imagined a middle-aged woman with a tight perm, flashing glasses and a thin, bony figure. "This is Mr. Macbeth," he said, appalled to hear his own voice sounding cringing and apologetic. "I won't be over today after all. I couldn't call you earlier because I was on a case."

"We've got enough to do here," snapped Maggie, "without having to cope with people cancelling appointments. I just wish that folk would tell the truth and say they're scared."

"I am not scared," howled Hamish. "Listen here. I haff the abscess in my tooth and the doctor says I will need to wait until the antibiotic works before seeing the dentist."

Maggie's voice was heavy with sarcasm. "Oh, and when is that likely to be?"

Hamish took a deep breath. He was suddenly determined to see this dentist with the unsavoury reputation and this horrible receptionist. "Tomorrow," he said firmly.

"There's a Miss Nessie Currie has cancelled at three. You can have her appointment."

"Thank you." Hamish slammed down the phone.

Nessie Currie and her sister, Jessie, were the village spinsters. It was their fussy, gossipy manner which damned them as spinsters in a country like Scotland where women who had escaped marriage were sometimes considered fortunate, a hangover from the days when marriage meant domestic slavery and a string of children.

He decided to go and call on Nessie.

Nessie and Jessie were working in their small patch of front garden where narrow beds of regimented plants stood to attention bordering a square of lawn. A rowan tree, heavy with scarlet berries, stood beside the gate as it did outside many Highland homes as a charm to keep the fairies, witches, and evil spirits away.

"There's that Hamish Macbeth," said Jessie. "Hamish Macbeth." She had an irritating habit of repeating everything.

Nessie straightened up and pulled off her gardening gloves, the sunlight glinting on her glasses. "We heard there was the burglary over at The Scotsman," she said. "Why aren't you over there?"

"Over there," echoed Jessie, pulling a weed.

"I'm working on it. Why did you cancel your dentist's appointment, Nessie?"

"It is not the criminal offence."

"Criminal offence," echoed the Greek chorus from the flower bed.

"Chust curiosity," said Hamish testily, his Highland accent becoming more pronounced as it always did when he was irritated or upset.

"I don't see it's any business of yours, but the fact is, Mr. Gilchrist has a reputation of being a philanderer and I was going to have the gas, but goodness knows, he might interfere with my person."

"Interfere with my person," said Jessie, sotto voce.

Hamish looked at Nessie's elderly and flat-chested body and reflected that this Gilchrist must indeed have one hell of a reputation.

He touched his cap and walked off. The sun was slanting over the loch and soon the early northern night would begin. He felt suddenly lonely and wished he could speak to Priscilla and immediately after that thought had a sudden sharp longing for a cigarette although he had given up smoking some years before.

"You're looking pretty down in the mouth." The doctor's wife, Angela, stopped in front of him. "Tooth still hurting?"

"No, it's fine at the moment. I was wishing Priscilla was back. We aye talked things over. Then the damnedest thing. I wanted a cigarette."

Angela smiled, her thin face lighting up. "Why is it everything you let go of, Hamish, ends up with your claw marks on it?"

"I haff let go," said Hamish crossly. "I wass chust thinking . . ."

"And I'm thinking you could do with a cup of tea and some scones. Come along, I'm on my way home."

As Hamish walked beside her, he suddenly remembered that Angela's home-baked scones were always as hard as bricks and his diseased tooth gave an anticipatory twinge.

The scones that Angela produced and put on the kitchen table looked light and buttery. "A present from Mrs. Wellington," she said.

Hamish brightened. Mrs. Wellington, the minister's wife, was a good cook.

He had two scones and butter and two cups of tea. But disaster struck when Angela produced a pot of blackberry jam and urged him to try another. Hamish buttered another scone, covered it liberally in jam, and sank his teeth into it. A red-hot pain seemed to shoot up right through the top of his head. He let out a yelp.

"I say, that tooth is hurting," said Angela. "Probably the jam. There's a lot of acid in blackberries. Here." She rummaged in a kitchen drawer and drew out a handful of new toothbrushes and handed him one. "Go to the bathroom and clean your teeth and rinse out your mouth well. Then come back and I'll give you a couple of aspirin."

Hamish grabbed the toothbrush and went into the long narrow bathroom. Two cats slept in the bath and another was curled up on top of the toilet seat. He ripped the wrappings off the toothbrush, brushed his teeth, found a mouthwash in the cabinet and rinsed out his mouth. By the time he returned to the kitchen, the pain was down to a dull ache. He gratefully swallowed two aspirin.

"I thought you would be over at The Scotsman Hotel," said Angela.

The cats had followed Hamish from the bathroom. One began to affectionately sharpen its claws on his trouser leg and he resisted an impulse to knock it across the kitchen. Angela was very fond of her cats and Hamish was fond of Angela.

"Jimmy Anderson is on the case so I'm off it. Blair's liver is playing up so Jimmy has dreams of glory."

Angela cradled her cup of tea between her thin fingers. "I'm surprised you haven't been called to that hotel before."

"Why?"

"I suppose I shouldn't be telling you this, but I heard a rumour that Macbean beats his wife."

"Neffer!"

"I think he does. She had bruised cheeks two months ago as if he'd given her a couple of backhanders."

Hamish leaned back in his chair and clasped his hands behind his head. "Now there's a thing. A battered wife and two hundred and fifty thousand pounds missing from the safe. She could get a long way away from him on that."

"Battered wives don't usually have the guts to do anything to escape. Not unless there's another man."

Hamish thought of the acidulous Mrs. Macbean with her thin, lipsticked mouth and hair in pink rollers and sighed. "No, I don't think it can be anything to do with her. Thanks for the tea and everything, Angela. I'd best get back to the station."

Jimmy Anderson was waiting for him. "Typed up your notes yet on that burglary?"

"You said you didn't want them."

"Well, I would like them now." Jimmy followed Hamish into the police station and through to the police office. "Got any whisky?"

Seeing that Jimmy was restored to something like his normal self, Hamish said, "Aye, there's a bottle in the bottom drawer. I'll get you a glass."

"What about yourself?"

"Not me," said Hamish with a shudder. "I have the tooth-ache."

"Get them all pulled out, Hamish. That's what I did. I got a rare pair of dentures. I even got the dentist to stain them a bit wi' nicotine so they look like the real thing."

He bared an evil-looking set of false teeth.

Hamish got a glass and poured Jimmy a generous measure of whisky.

"So what's happening with the burglary?"

Jimmy looked sour. "Nothing. We'll need to wait for the reports on Macbean and the staff to see if any of them has a criminal background."

"I hear Macbean beats his wife."

"This is the Highlands, man. What else do they do on the long winter nights?"

"Just thought I'd tell you, which is very generous of me, considering you sent me away wi' a flea in my ear. You had a touch of Blairitis."

"You'd best keep your ear to the ground, Hamish, or we'll have that pillock, Blair, poking his nose in."

"I'll see what I can do."

"Maybe you'd best go back there tomorrow."

And Hamish would have definitely gone straight to The Scotsman Hotel in the morning but for one thing. After he had typed out his notes for Jimmy, he found the whole side of his face was burning and throbbing with pain. He decided to go straight to Gilchrist and ask him to pull the tooth. He could make time between appointments. There was just so much pain a man could bear.

He got into the police Land Rover and set out on the narrow one-track road which led to Braikie. The weather was milder, which meant a thin drizzle was misting the windscreen and the cloud was low on the flanks of the Sutherland mountains.

Braikie was one of those small Scottish towns where Calvinism seems to seep out of the very walls of the dark grey houses. There was one main street with a hotel at one end and a grim-looking church at the other. Small shops selling limp dresses and food of the frozen fish fingers variety were dotted here and there. The police station had been closed down, Braikie having some time ago been considered near enough for Hamish Macbeth to patrol. But he hardly ever went there and had no reason to. Braikie might be a dismal place, but he could not remember a crime ever being committed there.

He asked a local where the dentist's surgery was and was told it was next to the church. It was situated above a dress shop where dowdy frocks at outrageous prices were displayed in the window, which was covered in yellow cellophane to protect the precious goods from sunlight, even though the dreary day was becoming blacker by the minute. The entrance to the dentist's surgery was a stone staircase by the side of the shop. He mounted slowly, holding his jaw although the pain had suddenly ceased in that mysterious way that toothache has of disappearing the minute you are heading for the dentist's chair.

He stopped on the landing and cocked his head to one side. It was quiet. No sound seemed to filter from inside.

A frosted-glass door with Gilchrist's name on it faced him. It was the only door on the landing.

With a little sigh, he pushed it open. The waiting room was empty, the receptionist's desk was empty. The silence was absolute. A tank of fish ornamented one corner, but the fish were dead and floating belly up. A table with very old copies of *Scottish Field* was in the centre of the room. Hard upright chairs lined the walls.

His tooth gave another sharp wrench of pain, and stifling a moan, he pushed open the surgery door.

A man was sitting in the dentist's chair, his back to Hamish. "Hullo," said Hamish tentatively. "Where's the dentist?"

Silence.

He strode around the front of the chair.

From the white hair and white coat, he realised he was looking at Mr. Gilchrist.

But his face was not white. It was horribly discoloured and distorted.

Hamish felt for a pulse at the wrist and then at the neck.

Mr. Gilchrist was dead.

CHAPTER TWO

My name is Death: the last best friend am I.

—Robert Southey

Hamish stood for a moment, shocked. And then the heavy stillness was broken, almost as if the whole of the small town had
been waiting for him to find the body.

A dog barked in the street below, its master called it in an
angry voice, an old car coughed and spluttered its way, and
high heels sounded on the stone staircase outside.

He heard the outside door opening as the high heels clacked
their way in. He opened the door of the surgery. A beautiful
girl was hanging her coat on a hatstand in the corner. She had
glossy jet black hair, a white clear complexion and large blue
eyes. She was of medium height with a curvaceous figure and
excellent legs. "What do you want?" she snapped, and, oh, the
voice did not match the face or figure. But the voice was undoubtedly that of the receptionist, Maggie Bane.

"Who are you?" she went on. Hamish was not in uniform.

"Hamish Macbeth."

"Well, Mr. Macbeth, Mr. Gilchrist has his coffee at this time in the morning and does not like to be disturbed."

"He's dead."

She did not seem to hear him. She detached a white coat from the coat rack and put it on. "In any case," she went on, "your appointment is for three o'clock this afternoon. Not eleven o'clock this morning."

"He's dead!" howled Hamish. "Mr. Gilchrist is dead and it looks like poison to me."

Those wide blue eyes dilated. She suddenly ran past him into the surgery. She stared down at the dead body of the dentist. She stood there in silence. She looked as if she might never move again.

"Miss Bane!" said Hamish sharply. "I am a police officer. Do not touch anything. I'll need to phone police headquarters."

He walked forward and took her by the shoulders and guided her back to her desk. "Sit down and don't move," he ordered.

She sat down numbly and stared straight ahead.

He dialled the Strathbane number and got through to Detective Chief Inspector Blair, who listened while Hamish quickly outlined the finding of the body. "I'll be over right away," said Blair in his heavy Glaswegian accent. "Trust you to find another body. If ah hadnae enough on ma hands as it is."

Hamish put down the receiver and turned to Maggie Bane. "Do you feel up to answering a few questions, Miss Bane?"

She sat motionless.

"Miss Bane?"

Those beautiful eyes finally focused on him. "I can't believe it," she whispered. "I took him in his morning coffee and went out to the shops. Oh, here's his next patient coming."

Hamish went quickly to the door. A woman stood there, holding a small child by the hand. "I'm afraid there's been an accident," he said. "I am a police officer. Give me your name and address and we will be in touch with you."

He coped with her startled questions as best he could, noted down her name, address and telephone number, and then went quickly into the surgery, where the dead body lay in the chair, to look for the coffee cup. He found it over by a stainless steel sink. Cup and saucer had been washed.

He went back to Maggie. "Did he usually wash his own cup and saucer after drinking his coffee?"

"No," she said in a shaky voice. "He just usually left it and I washed it for him and put it away in the cupboard."

"How long have you worked for him?"

"Five years."

"I'll need your home address and telephone number, Miss Bane. I do not want to distress you now with too many questions. When did Mr. Gilchrist start work?"

"At nine o'clock."

"And you?"

"The same."

"And was he in a good mood? No signs of depression or distress?"

"What? Oh, do you mean would he have committed suicide? No. He was the same as ever."

Hamish crossed to the outside door, opened it and hung a CLOSED sign which had been hanging on the doorknob on the inside of the door on the outside doorknob. "What I need at the moment before the contingent from Strathbane arrives is your appointment book. Who had the first appointment?"

"Someone from Lochdubh." She pulled forward the book. She seemed unnaturally calm now. "Mr. Archibald Macleod."

Archie, the fisherman, thought Hamish.

"And how long was he with the dentist?"

"He wasn't. He didn't turn up."

"Who did Mr. Gilchrist see before his coffee break?"

"A Mrs. Harrison."

"Mrs. Harrison from outside Lochdubh on the Braikie road?"

"Yes, her."

"But she was spreading scandal that Mr. Gilchrist had sexually interfered with her."

"She's a nut case. She was always hanging around him."

Hamish scratched his head in perplexity.

"Mr. Gilchrist must have known what she had been saying about him. Why on earth was he treating her?"

"She was a good-paying customer."

"Now, let's go over your own movements. When you came in at nine o'clock, Mr. Gilchrist was the same as ever. Mr. Macleod did not turn up. The next was Mrs. Harrison. What did she have done?"

"She had a tooth drawn."

"How long was she with him?"

"Half an hour."

"And so it was coffee break time. You took him in a cup of coffee?"

"Yes. At ten o'clock. I told him I was stepping out to buy a few things from the shops."

"Show me where the coffee things are kept."

She rose and went over to a low cupboard next to the tank of dead fish. "Why are these fish dead?" asked Hamish.

"I don't know. I followed all the instructions properly but they died a week ago."

Hamish looked into the depths of the murky tank. "You should have a filter and the tank should have been cleaned."

"I didn't want the things," said Maggie, crouching down by the cupboard. "It was Mr. Gilchrist's idea. When they died he ordered me to clear out the tank and throw the dead fish away but I told him to do it himself."

"And he agreed?"

"What does it matter now?" demanded Maggie in that sharp, ugly voice of hers. "He's lying dead next door."

"We'll get back to it later." Hamish bent down in front of the cupboard. "So this is where you keep the coffee things." There was a can of instant coffee and three cups and saucers and two spoons, a bowl of lump sugar, and a carton of milk. "I'd better not touch anything here until the forensic team arrives," he said.

He was itching to go out and ask if anyone had been seen entering the surgery after ten o'clock. But he did not want to leave her alone. "How many lumps of sugar did Mr. Gilchrist take in his coffee?"

"Six lumps."

"Six! There's a packet of biscuits at the back," he said, peering into the depths of the cupboard. "Gypsy Creams. Did he have any of them?"

"He usually had two with his coffee but he said he didn't want any biscuits this morning."

"Did he say why?"

Maggie Bane stood up and suddenly began to cry. Hamish got slowly to his feet. "You'd best go and sit down," he said, although he could not help wondering whether the tears were genuine or not. Maggie's ugly voice robbed her of femininity and any softness.

He went back into the surgery and stared down at the dead man. If he had been poisoned, and Hamish suspected he might have been, then the killer had waited in the surgery for him to die and then had taken the cup and saucer and washed both. Hamish shook his head. Had he been arranged in the chair after death? Surely a poisoned man would writhe and vomit, stagger to the door for help.

Wait a bit, he thought. He, Hamish, had arrived just after eleven. When he had felt the pulse, the body was still warm.

He went back to the reception. Maggie had stopped crying and had lit up a cigarette.

"You went out to buy some things," said Hamish, "and yet you didnae get back here until after eleven. A long coffee break. Did you always go out?"

"No, hardly ever."

"And was the coffee break always an hour?"

"No, half an hour."

"So what kept you?"

"There wasn't another patient expected until that woman and her child turned up, Mrs. Albert and wee Jamie."

"But you gave me the impression when I phoned for an appointment that he was busy all day."

"It's business," she said wearily. "Mr. Gilchrist didn't like his clients to know that he wasn't fully booked."

Police sirens sounded, coming down the street. "This is the lot from headquarters," said Hamish.

When Blair lumbered in, a heavyset man whose fat face always seemed to be sneering, accompanied by his sidekicks, detectives Anderson and MacNab, and then the forensic team, pathologist and photographer, Hamish hurriedly outlined what he had found, and then suggested he should go out and try to find out if anyone had seen anything.

"Aye, all right," growled Blair ungraciously. "We don't want you getting in the way o' the professionals."

Hamish went out onto the landing. The staircase led to an upper floor. A man was leaning over the banister, looking down.

"Whit's going on?" he asked.

Hamish went up the stairs. "There's been a bit of an accident. I am a police officer."

"Aye, I ken you fine. You're thon Hamish Macbeth from Lochdubh."

He was an elderly man, small, gnarled, wearing the odd mixture of pyjamas, dressing gown and a tweed cloth cap on his head.

"Come ben," he said as Hamish reached the upper landing. Hamish followed him into a small, neat flat.

"What is your name?"

"Fred Sutherland."

"Right, Mr. Sutherland, the situation is this. Mr. Gilchrist has been found dead."

"Murdered?"

"We don't know yet. Now, did you hear any odd sound from downstairs between ten this morning and eleven?"

"Nothing oot o' the way. Usual dentist's noises."

"But he didnae hae a customer between those hours. What do you mean, dentist's noises?"

"Just that damn drill. I've got the dentures. Had them for years. But I tell you, laddie, every time that drill goes, my false teeth ache."

"I'll be back," said Hamish and shot out the flat and hurtled down the stairs.

The surgery was crammed with police. Hamish shoved his way in and said to the pathologist, "Have you looked at his teeth?"

The pathologist, a tall, lugubrious man, looked up from his examination in surprise. "He's a dentist. He looks at other people's teeth."

"Chust look at them," begged Hamish, "afore rigour sets in too bad."

"I was just about to examine the mouth." The pathologist prised the mouth open and shone a torch into it.

Then he looked up at Hamish with a startled expression on his face. "How did you know about this?"

"Know about what?" howled Blair.

"A hole has been drilled in each tooth."

"After death?" asked Hamish.

"I do not know," said the pathologist slowly. "The face is discoloured, yes, but I would expect signs of a struggle and bruising."

"How did you . . . ?" began Blair.

But Hamish ignored him. "There's something else. If he had been poisoned wi' something, surely he would have writhed about. Could someone have lifted him off the floor after death, put him in that chair and drilled his teeth?"

"Could be."

Blair managed to interrupt. "How did you know the teeth had been drilled?"

"A wee man who lives above the surgery heard the drill going when Gilchrist was not supposed to have a patient."

"But someone could have dropped in."

"Aye, but I wass beginning to get the feeling the man might be hated."

"I'll go and see your wee man myself." Blair set off.

Hamish then went downstairs to the dress shop underneath. A bell clanged above the door when he opened it. A fussy little woman came forward to meet him.

"I am a police officer," began Hamish.

"What's all the row upstairs?"

"Mr. Gilchrist is dead."

She was a neat middle-aged woman with neat closed features and white hair in a rigid perm. "Oh, dear. Is there anything I can do to help? Was it a heart attack?"

"No. What is your name?"

"Mrs. Elsie Edwardson."

"And you own this dress shop?"

"Yes."

"Did you notice anyone going up the stairs to the dentists between, say, ten and eleven o'clock?"

"Is it murder?"

"We don't know yet."

"Well, let me think. Dear me, this is quite a bit of excitement for us all." Her eyes gleamed. "Nothing usually happens in Braikie. Nobody even knows where Braikie is. I once went on a holiday to Scarborough and people had not only not heard of Braikie, they'd never heard of the county of Sutherland. That receptionist, that bad-tempered girl, Maggie Bane, I saw her go out but I couldn't be sure of the exact time."

"Anyone going in?"

She shook her head. "I was pricing goods in the back shop most of the time."

"And did you hear any funny noises from upstairs?"

"Not that I remember."

A glare of white light lit up the shop windows. "Dear me, what is that?" asked Mrs. Edwardson.

"I think Grampian Television has arrived."

"Oh, the television! My wee shop on the telly! I'd best go and put a little more lipstick on." Mrs. Edwardson was now flushed and happy. "This is grand publicity for my shop."

Hamish looked at the depressing display in the window and privately thought that even if Princess Diana appeared in a gown bought from Mrs. Edwardson, it would not sell one of them.

"We'll be talking to you again," he said, but Mrs. Edwardson already had her compact out and was applying pink lipstick in the little mirror.

He continued with his interviews in the shops on either side, occasionally pursued by the local press who all knew him. The death of a dentist and in such gruesome circumstances would soon bring up the national newspapers and then the foreign ones. Blair would feel under pressure and Blair under pressure was a nasty sight.

At last he returned to the surgery. Blair was telling Maggie Bane she would need to accompany them to Strathbane for questioning. He obviously thought her the prime suspect. Hamish reported his lack of success and Blair grunted and then told him to go about the town and see what he could dig up on Gilchrist's background.

"Was he married?" asked Hamish.

"He was, but he got a divorce ten years ago."

"And where's the wife?"

"Down in Inverness."

"What's her name?"

"Nothing to do wi' you," said Blair truculently. "Now run along and see if you can dae anything useful."

As Hamish went back down the stairs again, Jimmy Anderson was coming up.

"The press are driving me fair mad," he grumbled.

"Listen," said Hamish, catching his arm as he would have sprinted past up the stairs, "what's the name of the ex-wife?"

"Jeannie Gilchrist."

"And whereabouts in Inverness can she be found?"

"She can be found by the Inverness police."

"No more whisky for you, Jimmy."

"Och, if you're that interested, she's at 851 Anstruther Road."

"Thanks."

"Hamish!" Jimmy called after him. "Don't you go near her or Blair'll have you off the force."

Hamish waved by way of reply and went out to the police Land Rover. He was determined to go to Inverness because his tooth had started to ache again. He would go to his own dentist and then he may as well call on Mrs. Gilchrist. Various camera flashes went off in his face as he drove off. He knew the press had an irritating way of photographing everyone and everything. The photos would not be used.

As he took the long road to Inverness, putting on the police siren so that he could exceed the speed limit, he reflected that it would be nice to be one of those private eyes in fiction before whose wisdom the whole of Scotland Yard bowed and who seemed to be kept informed of every step of the game. But he was only a Highland policeman, a little cog in a murder enquiry. Blair would get the pathologist's report and all the statements and he would need to winkle out what he could by plying Jimmy Anderson with whisky.

Once in Inverness, he went straight to his own dentist, a Mr. Murchison, and pleaded with the receptionist that the pain in his tooth was so bad he was about to die.

"They all say that," she said heartlessly. "Take a seat and I'll see if he can fit you in."

"Tell him I haven't much time," said Hamish with low cunning, for there were six people in the waiting room. "Mr. Gilchrist, the dentist over at Braikie, has just been murdered. And I am in the middle of a murder investigation."

"Oh, my! How dreadful. Wait there."

She went into the surgery. After a few moments, she emerged. "Mr. Murchison will see you right now. He's just finished."

A man walked out holding his jaw. Hamish walked in under the baleful stares of the waiting patients.

"What's this all about?" asked Mr. Murchison.

"It's this tooth here," said Hamish, opening his mouth.

"I mean about the murder?"

"Look, Mr. Murchison, just stop this pain and I'll tell you everything."

"All right. Get in the chair."

Half an hour later after draining the abscess, drilling the diseased tooth, and filling the hole, Mr. Murchison said, "Tell me all about it," and Hamish did the best he could although by that time half his face was still frozen with the injection.

"I'm not surprised," said Mr. Murchison at last. "I dealt with some of his ex-patients and I'd never seen such bad work. I'd just got together with some of my colleagues and I was going to report him to the Health Board."

"But do you know anyone in particular who would hate him enough to murder him?"

"Not a one. You know how it is, people say, 'I'll murder that bastard,' but they never actually go and do it."

"Someone did," said Hamish.

He settled his bill with the receptionist, complained bitterly about the price, wondering if these days the National Health Service actually paid for anything. Then he went out and drove out to Anstruther Road on the Loch Ness side of Inverness. He was just turning into Anstruther Road when he saw a police car. He swiftly reversed back around the corner. He got out and walked into Anstruther Road and then walked slowly up and down it until he saw a policeman and policewoman emerge from Mrs. Gilchrist's house, get into the car and drive off.

He walked towards the house, a trim Victorian villa, opened the gate and walked up to a front door with a stained-glass panel and rang the bell beside it.

The woman who opened the door came as a surprise to Hamish. She looked very young. She was wearing a blue T-shirt and blue jeans and her black hair was tied back in a ponytail. Her features were small and elfin.

"My name is Police Constable Macbeth," said Hamish. "Is Mrs. Gilchrist at home?"

"I'm Mrs. Gilchrist."

"Och, you look too young," Hamish blurted out.

Her face lit up in a charming smile. "I have just been interviewed by the police."

"I am from Lochdubh," said Hamish, "and I have just come from Braikie."

"You'd best come in, but . . ." She looked up at him doubtfully.

"But, what?"

"Have you been drinking?"

"No! Why . . . ? Oh, I've been to the dentist in Inverness, which is why my voice sounds slurred. My face is still frozen."

"I thought you sounded drunk. Come in, then."

Charming as Mrs. Gilchrist undoubtedly was, Hamish could not help noticing that the possible murder of her husband had left her unmoved.

The living room was designed in what he privately thought of as Scottish Modern: stripped pine furniture, lots of green plants, and prints by modern artists on the walls.

"Now Mrs. Gilchrist," said Hamish, "the death of your husband must have come as a great shock to you."

"Not really. I suppose the shock will hit me later."

"Did you divorce him or did he divorce you?"

"I divorced him."

"On what grounds?"

"I didn't like him," she said airily.

"Why?"

A look of irritation marred her pretty face. "It happens, you know. Little things begin to annoy and then they assume major proportions."

"Like what?"

"I don't see what this has to do with his possible murder."

Hamish sighed. "I'm trying to get a picture of your husband."

She echoed his sigh and then said, "I'll do my best. I was working in the council offices when I met him. He came in with some question about council tax. He asked me out for dinner, just like that. He seemed a very strong, definite person who knew where he was going and what he was doing and I was tired of being single. He was a lot older than I, fifteen years older, but that was part of the attraction. We got married a few weeks later. It became gradually clear to me that he was a petulant, arrogant man. Things that annoyed me? Oh, reading the newspaper aloud at the breakfast table and tutting over it and explaining how he could have managed the world better, criticising my clothes—he liked short skirts, high heels, little blouses, things like that. I said I would wear what I liked and the verbal abuse started. I began to feel demoralised. I had kept my job, thank God, and so I moved out to this place, and then got a divorce after two years' separation had passed."

"How old was he?"

"Fifty."

"Hadn't he been married before?"

"Yes, I think he had. But he was secretive about things. I just got a feeling he had."

"Where did he come from originally?"

"Dumfries."

Hamish studied her for a moment. Then he asked, "But just suppose this should turn out to be murder and I think it's bound to turn out that way, doesn't the idea startle you and shock you?"

"You must realise," she said gently, "that I came to hate him like poison. It stands to reason that some other woman would feel the same."

"I don't see that a woman would have the strength to watch him die, pick him up, put him in the dentist's chair, drill all his teeth and—"

"*What!*"

"Oh, dear, I thought the police that were here might have told you. But that's what seems to have happened."

"There must be some maniac on the loose."

"A very cold-blooded maniac. The surgery, I think, had been cleaned up."

"Do you mind leaving?" she said suddenly. "I don't think I can take any more at the moment."

Hamish walked to the door. Then he turned around. "Where were you this morning? Shouldn't you be at work?"

"I took the day off. Woman's troubles. Nothing too bad but my job bores me. No, I have no witnesses but I've been here all day till now."

As he drove off, the full enormity of the strange murder hit Hamish. There were so many questions he would like answers to. Why had Maggie Bane stayed away so long? What if someone like himself with an aching tooth had just decided to drop in? That CLOSED sign. He had handled it himself. Damn! What if the murderer had entered and just hung the sign outside the way he had done himself?

He drove straight to Braikie and parked on the outskirts of the town and then began to make his way on foot towards the dentist's surgery. A Strathbane policeman approached him. "Blair was going ballistic looking for you."

"I have been making the enquiries all over the town," said Hamish. "That man usually wants me off the case."

"Well, he said if I found you, you were to go straight to Strathbane. And he said to get your uniform on."

Hamish drove to Lochdubh, changed into his uniform, made

a sandwich and cup of coffee and then set out at a sedate pace for Strathbane. He did not like Blair. He did not like his anger or his bluster or the way he had of accusing the easiest person as a murderer. But when it came to everyday Strathbane crime, Hamish knew Blair to be good at his job. He kept his ear to the ground and knew all the villains.

The Land Rover crested a heathery rise and there below him lay Strathbane like the City of Dreadful Night. Black ragged clouds were racing across a windy sky and a fitful gleam of watery sunlight lit up the windows of the dreary tower blocks on the outskirts of the town.

Why such an excrescence should pollute the landscape of Sutherland, Hamish did not know. There had once been a lot of industry back in the fifties, paper mills, brick works, electronics factories, and the tower blocks had been thrown up to house the influx of workers from cities like Glasgow and Edinburgh. But the workers had brought their love of strikes north with them and gradually the following generations had preferred to live on the dole and not even pretend to work. Factories had closed down and the winds of Sutherland whipped through their shattered windows and fireweed grew in vacant lots. It was like one of those science-fiction movies about the twenty-first century where anarchy rules and gangs roam the streets. The last industry to go was the fishing industry, killed off by the European Union with its stringent fishing quotas and restrictions which only the British seemed to obey, and local lethargy. And then there were drugs. Drugs had crept north up the snaking new motorways which cut through the mountains: drugs like a plague, drugs causing crime; drugs breeding new white-faced malnourished children, AIDS from dirty shared needles, and death.

His jaw was beginning to ache from the punishment it had received at the dentist. He suddenly wished he had begged Mrs.

Gilchrist not to mention his visit to the Inverness police, for if Blair heard about it, he would treat it as a case of insubordination.

Hamish entered the gloomy building where the smells of food from the police canteen always seemed to permeate the stale air.

He opened the door of the CID room and peered through the haze of cigarette smoke. Jimmy Anderson was alone, puffing at a cigarette, sitting with his feet up on his desk.

"Oh, Hamish, man, you are in deep shite," he hailed him.

"Where's Blair?"

"Still interviewing Maggie Bane, suspect number one."

Hamish sat down opposite him. "Can I borrow this computer? I'd best start on my report."

"Help yourself. Where were you?"

"I was around Braikie, asking questions, and then went back to Lochdubh to change into my uniform," said Hamish, switching on the computer and then beginning to type his report of finding the body of Gilchrist.

"It looks as if you were right about one thing," said Jimmy laconically. "They guess there was poison in his morning coffee, he writhed and vomited, and fell on the floor. There were vomit stains on the back of his coat as if he had rolled in his ain sick. Someone cleaned him up as best they could, hoisted him into that chair, drilled his teeth, then cold-bloodedly washed the floor. There were traces of vomit in the cracks in the linoleum."

Hamish paused, his fingers hovering over the keys. "Why would anyone go to all that trouble?"

"What do you mean?"

"I mean, anyone with half a brain would have known we would have found the drilled teeth and the residue of vomit on the floor."

"Maybe the murderer was filled with blind hatred. Maybe he was so mad with rage, he didn't care whether he was interrupted or not."

Hamish shook his head.

"It took a steady hand to drill one neat hole in each o' his teeth. Anyone in a mad rage would have smashed all his teeth and then smashed the surgery."

"Could be. But the strength that it all took! That lets Maggie Bane out, I think."

"Unless," said Hamish, "she had an accomplice."

CHAPTER THREE

Bold and erect the Caledonian stood,
Old was his mutton and his claret good;
Let him drink port, the English statesman cried—
He drank the poison and his spirit died.

—John Home

Hamish typed away busily at his report. He remembered the day when computers were a deep and dark mystery to him. Now it was easier than a typewriter.

The door crashed open and Blair lumbered in. He loomed over Hamish. "Where were you?"

"I was interviewing townspeople," said Hamish, "and then I went to change into my uniform before reporting here." The printer rattled out the final page of his report. He bundled the pages together and handed them to Blair. "There's my report."

Blair took it and stood glaring. "Get to your feet, man, when a senior officer addresses you."

Hamish obediently stood up.

Blair suddenly sighed and slumped down in a chair. "Oh, sit

down, Macbeth," he grumbled, "and stop standing there looking as useless as you are."

Hamish sat down again. Jimmy sniggered.

"Where's Maggie Bane?" asked Hamish.

"Had to send her home," replied Blair with a surly scowl.
"I'll swear that lassie had something to dae with it, but she
sticks to her story."

"She said she was out shopping," said Hamish, "but she had
no bags of shopping with her when she returned to the
surgery."

"Oh, she had an explanation for that one. Says she went home
and left the stuff there. We checked at the shops she said she
went to and it all matches up. She went to the grocers and
bought stuff, paid the rental on her telly, borrowed two videos
from the video library and changed her books at the public library. It all checks out."

"But why this morning?" asked Hamish. "Did she usually
take an hour off?"

"She sticks to her story that it was a quiet morning and she
took advantage of it. She said she asked Gilchrist's permission
and he said it was all right. Och, the number of people that
need tae be interviewed. We've got tae see all his patients. Thon
Mrs. Harrison wasn't at home earlier. You can make yourself
useful and drop in on her and get a statement, and get one
from that fisherman, Archie Macleod."

"I thought the CID took statements in a murder enquiry,"
said Hamish.

This was indeed the case, but Blair, despite his insults, se-
cretly valued the lanky Highland policeman's intelligence. All
Blair's wits were usually put to using Hamish and at the same
time making it look as if any flashes of insight were his own.

"Was Gilchrist in debt, by any chance?" Hamish asked when
Blair's answer to his previous question had only been a belch.

"He wisnae robbed," howled Blair, his accent thickening as he grew more truculent. "Why d'ye ask?"

"Just an idea," said Hamish, heading for the door.

Night was falling on unlovely Strathbane as he left police headquarters. The orange sodium lights were staining the Highland sky where dirty seagulls who never seemed to sleep wheeled and screeched.

As he pulled up at a red light, a pinched-faced youth staggered and then gave the police Land Rover a vicious kick.

The light turned green and Hamish drove on, reflecting that if he arrested every yob in Strathbane who kicked a police car or spat on it it would mean he'd never have time for anything else.

The erratic wind of Sutherland had died. Frost was already beginning to sparkle on the road ahead. When he got to Lochdubh he drove straight through it and out onto the Braikie road where Mrs. Harrison lived. She would certainly have heard of the murder by now. The Highland tom-toms would have been beating from Sutherland to Caithness, to Inverness-shire and Ross and Cromarty.

He drew up outside a small, low croft house. There was a light shining from the window and a battered old Vauxhall parked outside. It looked as if Mrs. Harrison was at home. He hesitated, his hand on the gate. With Mrs. Harrison's reputation, they should have sent a woman.

But he shrugged and marched up to the low door and rang the doorbell. The door opened suddenly and a small woman looked up at him. Her hair was dyed black, that dead lifeless black, and her wrinkled skin was yellowish. Her dark eyes somewhere between black and brown glittered out over heavy pouches. Her thin, old, disappointed mouth was permanently turned down at the corners. She was wearing a dress which looked as if she had bought it from Mrs. Edwardson, and over it, a Fair Isle cardigan.

"It's the police, is it? It's about time you got here," she said. "Why aren't you in plain clothes?"

"Because I'm a policeman. May we go inside?"

"No, we may not. I have my reputation to think of."

Frost glittered on the branches of the rowan tree beside the door. Rowan trees were planted to keep the witches and fairies away, thought Hamish. Hadn't done its job with this house.

"Then you will need to accompany me to the station," he said severely. "You should not be obstructing the police in their enquiries."

"I'm too old to be cavorting about the countryside at this time o' night. You can come in."

He followed her into a living room cum kitchen. A peat fire burned in a black old-fashioned range along one wall. There was a table in the middle of the floor covered with a plastic cloth. Four hard upright chairs surrounded it. An oak sideboard stood against the wall opposite the fire containing photographs in silver frames. A picture of Billy Graham hung over the sideboard. There was no carpet on the stone-flagged floor.

He took off his peaked cap and placed it on the table and took out his notebook.

"Now, Mrs. Harrison," he began, "may I have your full name?"

"Mrs. Mabel Harrison."

"Age?"

"None of your business, young man."

"I need your age."

"I don't see why. Oh, well, fifty."

Probably nearer seventy, thought Hamish. Let it go for the moment.

"You went to see Mr. Gilchrist this morning and had a tooth drawn. Why did you go to Mr. Gilchrist? I believe you complained at one time that you suspected he had sexually assaulted you."

She gave him a coy look. "He didn't actually assault me. But he fancied me something bad."

"He made overtures to you?"

"There was the time I knew he was about to ask me out, but *she* came in and sat there and she wouldn't go away."

"Maggie Bane?"

"Calls herself a nurse and she's nothing more than a receptionist. She's jealous of me."

Why did I take this job, thought Hamish wearily. Why am I sitting in this cold kitchen listening to a madwoman?

"What was Mr. Gilchrist's manner like?"

"What do you mean?"

"Did he seem worried, frightened, hurried, anything like that?"

"No, he was the same."

"I do not think I can understand either you or the dentist," said Hamish. "You did put about stories that he had molested you because they were all over Lochdubh. He must have heard them. Why did you go, and why did he continue to treat you?"

"Can't you understand plain English?" she demanded nastily. "I've told you already. He fancied me."

"Suppose that to be the case, you did not notice anything odd in his manner?"

"No, he was the same and herself just sat there, reading a magazine."

"In the surgery?"

"Yes, the whole time I was there. Jealous bitch!"

"And did Maggie Bane say anything to Mr. Gilchrist or did Mr. Gilchrist say anything to Maggie Bane?"

"No . . . Wait a bit. He was just finished and he said to her, 'You can take yourself off when you see Mrs. Harrison out.'"

"And that was all?"

"Apart from the usual stuff, open wider, that sort of thing."

Hamish closed his notebook. "There will probably be a detective along to take another statement. Do not leave the country."

"Why did you say that, do not leave the country?"

"I always wanted to," mumbled Hamish, wondering in that moment whether he were not sometimes as deranged as Mrs. Harrison.

"Just drop back if there's anything else you want to know." She flashed a smile at him and he backed towards the door. Most of her teeth were missing. Had she needed all those teeth pulled or had the besotted old harridan used tooth pulling as a way to keep seeing a rapacious and greedy dentist? Extractions were less work than fillings and dentists could claim more from the National Health for them.

He turned in the doorway. "Just one more thing. You are a widow?"

"My Bill died twenty years ago almost to the day."

She walked to the sideboard and picked up a photograph. "That's me and Bill on holiday at Butlin's in Ayr."

A handsome young man with a pretty girl on his arm stared out of the frame. It was hard to believe that Mrs. Harrison had ever been as attractive as the girl in the picture. "What did your husband die of?" he asked, handing it back.

"A heart attack."

"Aye, well, I'd best be on my way."

He went back to the door and touched his cap and escaped out into the night where he stood for a moment at the gate and took in a deep breath of cold fresh air. The one curious thing about Mrs. Harrison's statement was the dentist telling Maggie she could go. Innocent enough, of course, if she had asked permission. Still . . .

He drove thoughtfully back to Lochdubh and parked outside the police station and then went down to the harbour where the fishing boats were preparing to set sail. Archie Macleod was possibly, because of his terrifying wife, the only fisherman ever to go to sea with a tight suit and a collar and tie under his overalls.

"It's yersel, Hamish," he said gloomily. "I thought you'd be along. It's about thon dentist?"

"Aye, why did you cancel, Archie?"

"Och, the pain wasnae that bad after all."

"Why Gilchrist, Archie? I mean, it seems the man doesn't have that much of a reputation."

"He's cheap," said the fisherman. "Man, the prices they charge these days. I can 'member getting the lot of the National Health."

Hamish took out his notebook and took down details of where Archie had been at the time of the murder. Archie, it transpired, had been in the Lochdubh bar with about fifty other locals to bear witness to the fact.

"They say someone drilled all o' his teeth," said Archie.

"How did you hear that? Was it on the news?"

"No, but Nessie Currie told Mrs. Wellington who was over shopping in Braikie and someone had told her." The Highland tom-toms *had* been beating, thought Hamish.

"Had you been to Gilchrist before?"

"No, never had trouble for years. As I say, someone told me he was cheap."

"Off you go, Archie. One more thing."

"Aye?"

"Do you wear that collar and tie and suit all the time you're out there?"

Archie grinned. "Take the damp things off as soon as I'm out o' sight o' the wife's binoculars."

Hamish grinned back and walked towards the police station. He was suddenly ravenously hungry. There was nothing in the police station larder but a few tins of things like salmon and beans. He decided to go to the Italian restaurant in the village, now managed by his once policeman, Willie Lamont. When Hamish had been briefly promoted to sergeant, Willie had worked for him. Willie had married a relative of the owner and settled happily into the restaurant business. He was a fanatical cleaner and although the Napoli, as the restaurant was called, had excellent food, the restaurant was always permeated by a strong smell of disinfectant.

Hamish entered and took a table by the window, the table where he usually sat with Priscilla when they went out for dinner together. There were few customers. He felt that stab of loneliness again.

Willie came up. "What's your pleasure, Hamish?"

"Just spaghetti and a salad, Willie. How's Lucia?" Lucia was Willie's beautiful wife.

"Doing just fine."

The restaurant door opened and a girl entered with a backpack on her shoulders. Willie frowned. He did not like hikers; he thought they lowered the tone of the place. Hamish knew that and said hurriedly, "Don't be hassling her, Willie. The place is quiet tonight."

"Yes, miss?" demanded Willie. "Careful with that backpack of yours. I don't want you knocking things off the tables. You'd best leave it outside."

"What if someone steals it?" asked the girl.

"You've got the police in here."

"But my rucksack would be outside," she said reasonably.

"I am afraid all the tables are reserved," said Willie.

Hamish stood up. "In that case, miss, you're welcome to share my table." He glared at Willie.

Reassured by the police uniform, she said, "Thanks." He helped her off with her backpack and put it on the floor in the bay of the window. She was wearing a woolly hat which she pulled off. Glorious thick brown curly hair tumbled about her shoulders. "Is there a toilet here? I want to take this off. It's pretty hot." She indicated the one-piece scarlet ski suit she was wearing.

"Over in the corner," said Hamish.

He waited until she had disappeared and then put his head round the kitchen door and shouted, "Willie!"

Willie came up wiping his hands on his apron.

"Cancel my order."

"You leaving?"

"No, I want to see what she orders. I might buy her dinner."

"And you that could have had Priscilla Halburton-Smythe, slumming wi' a hiker."

"Aw, shut up, Willie. You were neffer such a snob when you were a policeman."

He retreated back to the table.

When the girl reappeared, her ski suit over her arm, Hamish got respectfully to his feet.

She had put makeup on her pretty face. She had wide grey eyes and all that beautiful hair. Her mouth was small, soft and well-shaped. She was now wearing a tailored white blouse and black, tight-fitting trousers. She had a gold watch on one wrist.

"You are very kind, officer," she said in a beautiful, well modulated voice. "I am sure these tables are not reserved. That snobby waiter just doesn't like hikers."

"Pay no heed. Willie's the local eccentric. You needn't call me officer. I'm not on duty." He held out his hand. "My name's Hamish—Hamish Macbeth."

She shook his hand. "I'm Sarah Hudson."

"You're obviously English, Miss Hudson . . ."

"Sarah."

"Sarah. What brings you to the Highlands?"

"I felt like getting away from London—as far as possible. So I just took off."

Willie appeared with menus. He looked taken aback at Sarah's new appearance.

"As a matter of fact, miss," he said, "I've just realised I do have a free table."

"Miss Hudson is my guest," said Hamish firmly.

"Oh, that's very kind of you," said Sarah, "but I couldn't possibly . . ."

"I insist," said Hamish. They studied the menus. "I think we'll have a bottle of wine, Willie. The Valpolicella, if that suits you, Sarah?"

"Lovely. Do you know I think I'll just have a big plate of spaghetti bolognese and some garlic bread and a green salad."

"The same for me, Willie," said Hamish.

"May I smoke?" asked Sarah.

"Oh, yes," said Willie. "I'll get you an ashtray right away." Just as if, thought Hamish amused, Willie had not tried to have smoking banned in the restaurant. But the Highlands of Scotland were like the Third World when it came to cigarette smokers and the owner had insisted on allowing smoking.

"How's crime?" asked Sarah when Willie had left.

Her eyelashes were really ridiculously long, thought Hamish. He realised he was staring at her and said quickly, "Pretty bad."

She laughed. "I thought this place would be famous for its lack of crime."

"We had the murder today."

"In the village?"

"No, but nearby. A town called Braikie about twenty miles north."

"Who was murdered?"

"The dentist," said Willie eagerly, who had reappeared with a bottle of wine. "Terrible it was."

"Chust pour the wine, Willie," said Hamish crossly, "and I'll tell Miss Hudson about it. It iss not as if you are on the force anymore."

"I am sure I did not mean to be obstructive," said Willie huffily.

"Obtrusive, Willie." Hamish sipped some of the wine. "Yes, that'll do nicely."

When Willie had left again after placing a large glass ashtray in front of Sarah, she lit a cigarette. Hamish fought down a sudden impulse to ask for one. "So go on," she said. "Tell me about the dentist."

So Hamish told her all about the pain in his tooth, the visit to the dentist, the discovery of the body, the drilled teeth, everything he knew.

"How bizarre!" she said when he had finished. "But surely it's all very odd. Look here. Anyone could have walked in. And why did that receptionist stay away so long? It looks to me as if he expected a visit from someone he wanted to be private with and so he told the receptionist to take a long break."

"But she would need to know who it was and why she was meant to stay away," Hamish pointed out. "Otherwise why didn't she say how unusual it all was? Yet, she just sticks to her story that it was a quiet day and she had a lot to do."

"Oh, here's our food." She stubbed out her cigarette. They ate in silence for a bit.

Then Hamish asked, "Was there any particular reason why you arrived in Lochdubh, or were you just wandering about the Highlands?"

"I was coming here anyway. A friend of mine in London said it was a lovely place. I work for a financial consultants in the

City. I usually go on holiday abroad. But this year—well, I've had a bit of trouble—I felt like some healthy exercise."

"What's the name of your friend?"

"Priscilla Halburton-Smythe."

Hamish's poor heart gave a lurch. "Did she mention me?"

"No, she mentioned her family ran a hotel here. I said I would be backpacking, so I'd probably stay at some bed-and-breakfast. Can you recommend one?"

"There's several in the village. They don't usually take guests in the winter. The Tommel Castle Hotel isn't all that expensive in winter and you'd be comfortable there. I can take you up after dinner, if you like?"

"I think I'll do that. I've been walking for ages now and I could do with some comfort. There's not all that much privacy in a bed-and-breakfast. The last one I stayed in was full of shrieking kids." She smiled at him, a glorious smile, and the sharp pain Hamish had felt at the mention of Priscilla's name disappeared like Scottish mist before warm sunlight.

"So tell me more about this murder," she went on. "There must be press everywhere."

"Yes, they'll be around for a bit. Nothing had happened here for a while. First there was a burglary. Two hundred and fifty thousand pounds was stolen from the safe at The Scotsman Hotel and now this."

"Sin bin of the north!"

"Aye, you could say that. Wait a bit . . . there's a thing."

"What?"

"Macbean, the manager of The Scotsman—his wife and daughter were over at that dentists yesterday. Damn, I was supposed to go over there today but the murder drove it out of my head."

"Do you think there could be a connection?"

"No, but Macbean's wife or daughter might have heard or seen something."

"So might any of the other patients. All you have to do, surely, is pick out all the names and addresses from the dentist's files and go through them one by one."

"The headquarters at Strathbane will be doing that. I just interview who I'm told to interview." And please God, Blair doesn't find out about that visit to Inverness. "I'll go over first thing in the morning."

They moved to other subjects. She told him about working in London but nothing about her personal life. She did not mention Priscilla again and Hamish was damned if he would ask about her. He did not want to spoil this pleasant evening with this glorious girl.

After dinner, which he insisted on paying for, despite her protests, she disappeared back to the toilet to put her ski suit on, then with Hamish carrying her rucksack, they left the restaurant. "Just wait here and I'll get the Land Rover," said Hamish. He wasn't supposed to drive passengers around in it unless they were suspects, but he would be safe from Blair for the rest of the night.

At first, he thought she had gone and felt quite dismal, but then she stepped out of the shadows at the side of the restaurant. He helped her in and then drove off. She was wearing some sort of exotic perfume which she certainly had not been wearing earlier. He hoped she had put it on for him.

At the hotel, he introduced her to Mr. Johnson and begged for a cheap room for her.

"Miss Hudson, Macbeth is the village moocher," said Mr. Johnson, "but he says you're a friend of Priscilla's so we've got a wee room which is reasonable."

"I'll be on my way then," said Hamish awkwardly. He desperately wanted to ask her when he could see her again, but felt suddenly shy.

"My turn to take you for dinner tomorrow, Hamish," said Sarah. "Eight o'clock?"

His hazel eyes lit up. "Aye, that would be grand."

She kissed him on the cheek and said good night. He walked out in a happy dream, a silly smile on his face.

The frost sparkled on the ground and the stars sparkled overhead and it was like Christmas. He had not felt quite so happy or elated in ages.

He awoke next morning with a feeling of anticipation. Then he remembered that dinner date. But work first. He set out on the Lairg road for The Scotsman Hotel.

It had the deserted, shabby air of a second-rate Scottish hotel in winter. The wind was blowing again, sending the clouds racing across the sky, but it was unusually mild. The air felt damp against his cheek heralding the advance of rain.

He went into the hotel. The barman, Johnny King, was unloading crates of beer.

"Where's Mr. Macbean?" asked Hamish.

Johnny jerked his head in the direction of the office. Macbean was sitting at his desk.

"Where's the safe?" asked Hamish.

"Your boys took it away," said Macbean. "Fat lot o' good that'll do."

"You couldn't have been thinking of repairing the back and using it again!"

"No," said Macbean shiftily. "But I'm going down to Inverness tomorrow to get a new one. What do you want? I've been answering questions till I'm sick o' them."

Hamish removed his hat and put it on the desk and sat

down on a chair opposite Macbean. "I've really called in the
hope of seeing your wife and daughter."

"Why?"

"Did you hear about this murder over at Braikie?"

"Aye."

"Your wife and daughter went to see Gilchrist. I would be
interested to hear what they thought of him."

"They're somewhere about. They cannae tell you anything."

"I chust want an idea of what sort of man Gilchrist was."

Macbean snorted with contempt. "When you're in the dentist's chair getting a tooth pulled, do you sit there and wonder
what kind of man he is?"

"Yes," said Hamish Macbeth, whose Highland curiosity
prompted him to speculate on the character of everyone he
came across.

"I'll get someone to find them for you."

"About the money," said Hamish. "Were you insured against
theft?"

"Yes."

"To the tune of two hundred and fifty thousand pounds?"

"Yes, I made a point of paying heavy insurance to cover any
possible theft of the bingo money."

"So that means you'll be able to have the big night after all?"

"Sometime or another when the insurance company finishes
its investigations and gets around to paying."

"I should think," said Hamish, "that they might consider a
safe with a wooden backing an invitation to crime. Are you sure
you'll get your money?"

Macbean's eyes blazed with anger. "I'd bloody well better get
it. How will the insurance company know the safe had a wood
back anyway?"

Was he really this stupid, wondered Hamish.

"They'll get all the police reports and then they'll send their own investigators. Then the company who owns this hotel will want to know why you had such an unsafe safe."

The anger left Macbean's eyes and he groaned. Then he said, "Look, if you want to talk to the wife, run along and do it, and stop worrying me with these questions. Ask Johnny to find them."

Hamish rose and picked up his cap and put it under his arm and went out of the office to where Johnny was still unloading bottles of beer.

"I want to talk to Mrs. Macbean and her daughter," he said.

"I'll get them."

The barman picked up a phone on the bar and dialled an extension number. "Police tae see you, Mrs. Macbean, and Darleen," he said. The voice quacked on the other end of the line.

The barman replaced the receiver. "Give her a few minutes."

"Any ideas about who might have stolen the money?" asked Hamish.

"Naw. Why shoulda?"

"You surely must have discussed it with the other members o' the staff."

"Let me tell you somethin'," said Johnny, lifting a crate with strong tattooed arms, "I keep masel' tae masel.' You can ask the others if you want any gossip."

He turned his back on Hamish and walked off to the nether regions, carrying the crate.

It was an odd place for a bar, thought Hamish, placed as it was along one wall of the reception area like a theatre bar.

There was a clack of heels and Mrs. Macbean and her daughter, Darleen, came in. Mrs. Macbean was wearing yellow plastic rollers in her hair this time. Hamish wondered wildly if she ever took them out and if they were colour coordinated to match her clothes, for she was wearing a sulphur yellow blouse. Darleen was in jeans with frayed slits at each knee, a satin pyjama jacket, but no makeup, which made her look much younger.

"I'm sick o' the police," began Mrs. Macbean. "Questions, questions, questions."

"This will not take long," said Hamish soothingly. "Is there somewhere we can sit down and talk?"

She led the way through a pair of double doors leading off the main reception area. He found himself in a rather sleazy dining room with the residue of breakfast still lying about on three tables. "I see you have guests," said Hamish. "I assume the police have questioned them?"

"They've questioned everyone in the whole bloody place."

She sat down at a table. Darleen sat down next to her, crossed her long legs and winked at Hamish. Hamish took out his notebook and sat down as well.

"Now the morning of the burglary, you and Darleen had been over at the dentists in Braikie. You know the dentist has been found murdered. So I am trying to get a picture of what sort of man Gilchrist was. Had you been to him before?"

"Ma got her dentures from him," said Darleen and Mrs. Macbean glared at her daughter.

"A dentist is just a dentist," she complained. "You don't wonder about anything but getting your teeth out."

So much for progress, so much for cleaning and flossing, so much for dental technology, thought Hamish. This was still Scotland. Out with all of them and get yourself a nice set of false teeth.

"What about you, Darleen?" he asked.

Darleen giggled. "He was dead sexy."

"In what way?"

"He used tae stroke my hair and tell me I was a good girl. Cool."

"Pay no heed to her," snapped Mrs. Macbean. "She thinks everything in trousers is after her."

"And they usually are," commented Darleen, smug in the security of long legs and youth.

"Did either of you ever meet him socially?"

"What d'ye mean?" Mrs. Macbean lost a roller.

"I mean, did he ever ask either of you out on a date?"

"Here!" screeched Mrs. Macbean. "What are you getting at? You cannae solve a burglary and now you're trying to pin a murder on me."

"Och, no," said Hamish soothingly, wondering if her husband beat her out of a mixture of exasperation and hate—if he beat her. "Did you see anyone while you were at the surgery who looked as if they might loathe the man enough to murder him?"

"Everyone loathes the dentist."

"And you Darleen?"

"There was that awful old Harrison woman always hanging around. She gave me the creeps."

"Anyone else?"

"Naw."

"Look, we've got a hotel to run, copper." Mrs. Macbean got to her feet. She shook her head angrily and rollers fell from her head and rattled across the carpet, thick as autumnal leaves that strow the brooks in Vallombrosa. Hamish wondered whether to pick them up for her, but she was already walking away, leaving the rollers spinning across the carpet.

She turned in the doorway. "Come on, Darleen!"

Darleen winked at Hamish again and walked out after her mother, her hips swaying.

Hamish, who had stood up when they had left, sat down again and looked bleakly at the tablecloth, which had a large coffee stain in the middle of it although it was supposed to be clean. His mind wandered off to speculate on the various claims of washing powders, beaming women holding up stained items and then pulling them out of the machine an hour later with cries of joy. This cloth had come back from the laundry, starched and ironed but with the coffee stain still on it.

He jerked his mind back to the problem in hand. It was his own fault for doggedly avoiding promotion that he was kept in the dark as to what everyone had said in their statements. Had the dentist been sexy or had Darleen just been winding him up? What would a girl that young see in a middle-aged dentist? It was hard to tell what Gilchrist had really looked like. Had the pathologist's report come through?

Perhaps the day had come when he should alter his attitude to his job, apply for a job in the CID. But being a detective would mean moving to the hell that was Strathbane and working closely with Blair. Gone would be lazy days in Lochdubh. Was there something missing in his character, for he knew himself to be that rare thing, a truly unambitious man.

If this burglary had been an inside job, who was there on the inside? The staff of the hotel and the Macbeans. Was Macbean in debt? So many questions. He could go to Strathbane and try to get hold of Jimmy Anderson. But Blair would hear he had been at police headquarters and go through another of his lightning changes of mood and banish him from both cases.

Rain began to patter against the windows and the wind howled in increasing ferocity. The wind of Sutherland started with a regular gale and then increased to a booming sound finally ending in a great screech that rent the heavens from end to end. No wonder the locals were superstitious.

Was there any point in plodding on, finding out a bit here and a bit there? Why not go back to the police station, light the fire and settle down in front of it with a detective story, preferably an American one of the more violent kind where the hero could act out Hamish's frustrations for him, slamming people up against walls and beating confessions out of them.

But Duty, stern daughter of the voice of God, niggled at his conscience. He would go back to Braikie and see what he could find out there.

Starting with Maggie Bane.

Maggie Bane lived in a trim bungalow on the outskirts of Braikie called My Highland Home.

Hamish, as he rang the doorbell, wondered whether he should have called at the surgery first. But surely she would not be there. The police would have the whole place sealed off.

Maggie Bane answered the door and her face fell when she saw him. "I'm sick of the police," she said harshly.

"Just a few more questions," said Hamish soothingly.

"But two detectives have already been here this morning," she wailed. "And yesterday, that horrible fat man, Blair, kept shouting at me and did everything but charge me."

"It's like this, Miss Bane. It's a murder enquiry and I am sure you would be happy if we found the murderer. I think the answer to the murder must surely lie in Mr. Gilchrist's personality and who he knew, and who better to tell us than yourself?"

She fidgeted on the doorstep and then said reluctantly, "You'd better come in."

She led the way into a living room. It was furnished with a three-piece suite covered in flowered chintz. There was an electric fire, two bars, the kind that eats up electricity, the kind everyone in the Highlands bought in the heady days when they blocked off their coal fires under the impression that the Hydro Electric Board was going to supply cheap electricity. I mean, it all came from water, didn't it? Too late they found themselves faced with some of the highest electricity charges in Britain and yet the electric fires remained and the coal fires stayed blocked up. Women in the Highlands, it seemed, did not want to go back to the days of shovelling coal and raking out ashes. There was a noisy flowered wallpaper on the walls, bamboo poles with writhing green vegetation. There was a square dining table at the window with a bowl of artificial flowers on it. A low coffee table stood in front of the sofa, with glossy magazines arranged in neat piles, rather like in a waiting room.

"Coffee?" she asked.

"No, thank you," said the normally mooching Hamish, but he was anxious to get down to business.

She began to cry. "You think I'm a suspect," she said when she could. "The police never take hospitality from people they think are guilty."

"Och, no," said Hamish. "I'm too anxious to get on with the questions, that's all. You go and dry your eyes and make us a cup of coffee."

Maggie gulped and nodded. She was a beautiful girl, he thought, when she had left the room, but with such an ugly voice, such an aggressive voice. She wasn't aggressive at the moment and again he had an uneasy feeling that Maggie Bane was maybe one of those women who could cry at will.

He looked around the room for any sign of a desk, but there was not even a sideboard or cupboard which might house letters or documents.

Now, if he was one of the detectives in the stories he liked reading, he would seduce her and when she was asleep, search her bedroom and handbag. He grinned to himself. From his experience, he would probably sleep like a log and have to be awakened by her.

After some time, he was just beginning to wonder if she had run away, when the door opened and she came in carrying two mugs of coffee on a tray with milk and sugar.

"Were you fond of Mr. Gilchrist?" asked Hamish, once he was handed a mug of coffee.

"He was a good boss."

"He was divorced. Was he going with anyone?"

"He liked the ladies, but I do not think there was anyone in particular."

"And what about you, Miss Bane? Are you engaged?"

She held out one slim left hand. "See? No rings."

Hamish took a deep breath. "Were you at any time romantically involved with Mr. Gilchrist?"

She flushed angrily. "No, I was not!"

"I'm bound to hear if you were," said Hamish gently. "You know what it's like up here."

"We went out for dinner once or twice. You know how it is. Some days were very busy and it seemed natural for both of us to have a bite to eat before we went home."

Hamish made a mental note that there had probably been something going on. Gossip would already have been running rife all over the Highlands. At first people would be discreet because the man was so recently dead, but within a few more days tongues would begin to wag.

"Have you any idea why someone would hate him so much to kill him?"

She shook her head. "I think it was just some maniac who came up when I was out."

"Ah, about your going out. You have probably been questioned about that, but I must ask you again—why so long and why on that particular day?"

"I'm sick of this!" she said, her ugly voice rasping across the neat impersonality of her living room. "It was a quiet day. It was a chance to do my shopping. That's all."

"Are your parents alive, Miss Bane?"

"Yes."

"And where are they?"

"Dingwall."

"They must be concerned about you. Have they been to see you?"

"I haven't had much to do with them since I left university."

Hamish looked surprised. "Which university?"

"St. Andrews. I got a scholarship."

"Did you stay the full course? Did you get a degree?"

"Yes, I studied maths and physics."

Hamish leaned back in his chair and studied her thoughtfully. "And you worked for Gilchrist for five years! That must ha' been about your first job. Why should an attractive and highly educated young woman go to work for a dentist in a small town in Sutherland?"

"There are not many jobs around and just because one has a degree, a good job doesn't automatically follow."

"Yes, but . . ."

"Constable Macbeth," said Maggie firmly, getting to her feet, "I do not think you realise how tired and upset I am. I am in no fit condition to answer any more questions today."

Hamish rose as well. He looked at her thoughtfully. "I'll be back."

When he left, he half turned at the garden gate. So many questions unanswered. The main question was why she had buried herself in a dull town like Braikie, working as receptionist to a dentist with a bad reputation.

For the first time, he felt like giving up and letting Strathbane get on with it. What could one Highland constable do who did not have access to all the information, all the statements? He did not even know how Gilchrist had been killed.

CHAPTER FOUR

I regard you with an indifference closely bordering on aversion.

—Robert Louis Stevenson

Hamish parked the car at the police station, locked his hens away for the night, checked on his sheep, and then went for a walk along the waterfront in the watery greenish light of the Highland gloaming. The little waves of the sea loch, calmer now that the wind had moderated, slapped at the pebbled shore. A phone box by the harbour seemed shockingly scarlet in the soft gloom and muted colours of its surroundings. There were smells, of tar and fish, and diesel mixing with smells of cooking and strong tea as the villagers prepared their evening meals.

The lights of television sets flickered behind cottage windows, bringing the outside world to Lochdubh where villagers probably studied the latest fighting in Somalia with indifferent eyes while they talked about more interesting death close at hand.

"Hamish!" The voice was loud and peremptory. Mrs.

Wellington, the minister's wife, marched towards him. She was armoured in tweed, as usual, and on her head was a green felt hat with a pheasant's feather stuck in the hatband.

He looked wildly around, seeking some avenue of escape, but he was in full view of her.

She came up to him, her bulldog face heavy with accusation. "What are you doing about this dreadful murder?"

"I'm doing the little a Highland policeman can. If you have any complaints, you should talk to the superintendent, Mr. Peter Daviot."

"It's on your beat. You've solved cases before."

Hamish touched his cap. "I am doing what I can," he said, and then he walked quickly away.

And then he felt a little surge of gladness beginning somewhere deep inside him and realised he had that dinner date with Sarah. Time to put murder and mayhem out of his mind.

He went back to the police station, had a bath and dressed carefully in an elegant suit he had bought in a thrift shop, a striped shirt and a silk tie Priscilla had bought him. It was then he realised that his one pair of good shoes were in need of repair and he had forgotten all about it. The sole of the left one was hanging loose. He swore under his breath and got a tube of Stickfast Glue to effect an amateur repair. But the glue stuck to his fingers and his fingers stuck to the dangling sole of the shoe and there was no way he could get his fingers loose without tearing off skin.

In despair, he phoned the doctor's number and when Angela had stopped laughing, she said she would drop in and see what she could do.

Hamish glanced anxiously at the clock. He had spent a long time getting ready and it was now a quarter to eight. When Angela knocked at the kitchen door, he called, "Come in!" and went to meet her. She giggled at the sight of Hamish still glued to the sole of the shoe. "What am I to do?" demanded Hamish, exasperated.

"Sit down and don't panic," said Angela soothingly. She guided him to a kitchen chair. "Nail varnish remover should do the trick."

She fished in a capacious handbag and brought out a bottle of nail varnish remover and a packet of cotton balls. She soaked one of the balls in the remover and worked busily until Hamish found his hand free.

"Angela, you're a wonder. I'd better just put my boots on."

"Your police boots, Hamish? I hope it's not a heavy date. Oh, I know, it's that pretty girl who's staying up at the Tommel Castle Hotel."

"How did you know that?"

"Willie told everyone."

"Willie would," said Hamish bitterly. "No one will notice my boots. I'm meeting her at the restaurant. My feet will be under the table."

"How's that murder case?"

"I wouldnae know, Angela. They say, go and interview Miss or Mrs. so-and-so and I go and type up my report, but I never see the other statements."

"Gilchrist was having an affair with Maggie Bane."

"How did you find that out?"

"Highland gossip."

"Not very reliable. Good-looking woman. Always gossip."

"I cannot reveal my source, copper, but it's a pretty reliable one. Red-hot passion which seemed to be cooling off recently. They had a noisy scene in a pub down in Inverness about two months ago. Maggie was weeping and he was looking irritated."

"And someone from Lochdubh happened to be in the pub at the time?"

Angela nodded.

"But Maggie Bane! I would have thought it a cold-blooded murder by a pretty powerful man or men. That's it! It might have been more than one person."

Angela looked around the kitchen. The sink was piled high with dirty dishes and the table was covered with dirty coffee cups.

"I hope you aren't planning on bringing her back here, Hamish. The place looks like a slum."

Hamish coloured. "I haff had my mind on the other things."

"I'd help you, but I have to get back and put dinner on the table."

Hamish looked at his watch and let out a squawk of alarm. "Thanks, Angela. I'll need to hurry or I'll be late."

Soon he was heading along the waterfront in the direction of the restaurant, feeling his regulation boots getting bigger and clumsier by the minute.

Sarah was already there and seated at the table by the window. She was wearing a scarlet wool dress and an expensive pair of ruby and gold earrings.

Hamish, struck afresh by her beauty, felt suddenly shy.

"I'm sorry I'm a few minutes late," he said, sitting down opposite her. "I was on this murder case."

"Oh, how's that going?"

Willie came up with menus. They both ordered, and when Willie had left, Hamish said ruefully, "I'm not doing very well. Och, I may as well tell you. My one pair of good shoes had the sole hanging loose on one of them and a tried to stick it with Stickfast Glue and got stuck to the damn thing and had to wait for the doctor's wife to come and free me."

Sarah laughed. "I did notice the big boots when you came in the door and thought you'd forgotten to change them."

"I don't often dress up," said Hamish. A picture of Priscilla came into his mind and he looked out the window. In that moment, she felt so near to him that he half expected to see her walking along outside.

Sarah looked at his sad face curiously and then said, "This case is getting you down."

"You could say that. It's the first time I've felt so frustrated at being an ordinary copper who's kept out of things. Before I've found out the pathologist's report by phoning up and pretending to be Detective Chief Inspector Blair. I've found out about statements by plying another detective with whisky, but somehow I can't be bothered pulling any of those tricks again."

She studied him for a few moments and then asked, "Do you have a computer at the police station?"

"Yes, we're all computerised now."

"Did I tell you my job with the consultancy firm?"

"No, I thought you advised people on finances."

"I'm a systems analyst. That's how I met Priscilla. I was giving lectures on computers a few years ago at a business college."

Willie brought their food. He hovered around the table after he had served it, obviously hoping to be included in their conversation, but the restaurant was busy that night, and so he soon moved off.

"How is Priscilla?" asked Hamish.

"Very well as far as I could gather. Lots of social life."

"Got a steady boyfriend?"

"She's been seen around with a stockbroker."

Hamish picked at his food.

"Was there something between you and Priscilla?" she asked gently, after studying his downcast face.

"No, no," he lied. He suddenly wanted to forget about Priscilla. Her ghost was ruining the evening.

She wound a piece of tagliatelle neatly round her fork. "I might be able to help you."

"What do you mean?"

"Just suppose I could hack into the main computer at police headquarters, would you think that was illegal?"

Hamish's face brightened. "Och, no. I mean I am a policeman. I'm on this case in a way. It would save me a lot of bother. Could you do that?"

"I don't know. I could try."

"That would be grand." Hamish suddenly remembered the mess his home was in, but he thought that if he put her off and left it until the following day, she might change her mind.

"What is your superior officer like and what is his name?" asked Sarah.

"That's Detective Chief Inspector Blair, a Glaswegian, thick neck, trouble with booze, nasty. Wants me to solve cases for him but disnae want to give me any information unless he has to. I don't want to spoil this nice evening talking about him. Do you have a steady boyfriend?" he asked.

"No." That no was abrupt and the shutters were down over her eyes.

He said quickly, "Have you been this far north before?"

"Do you know, this is the first time I've ever been in Scotland, let alone this far north. It's another world, isn't it? I've walked in parts of Sutherland where you can look right and left and see nothing made by man. It's a scary feeling, like being on another planet. And the wind up here frightens me. You're walking along on a still day, then there's a little breeze and then without warning, a full gale hurtles out of nowhere, shouting and yelling and racing across the heavens. You walk forward against it at an angle while it tears at you like a live thing. And then it suddenly dies as abruptly as it had sprung up."

"When do you plan to move on?"

"In a few days' time. I must confess it's wonderful to have comfort again. But all the walking has done me good. It's a relief to get away from everything."

They ate in companionable silence for a while and then she asked, "Why do people kill people?"

"If it's Strathbane, then ten to one it's because of drink or drugs. Mostly domestic. Husband gets drunk and comes home and beats his wife and doesn't know when to stop. But when it's a murder in a small town, then it's usually passion or money."

"And what do you think it is in this case?"

"I don't know enough. It turns out that the dentist's receptionist, Maggie Bane, might have been having an affair with him. But she couldn't have committed the murder because she went out to do some errands between ten and eleven o'clock."

"Could the murder have been done before then?"

He shook his head. "Gilchrist had a patient, a Mrs. Harrison, just before Maggie Bane went out. He was alive and well at ten o'clock."

"I would like to get started," she said. "You can give me coffee at the police station."

Curious Highland eyes watched them leave. Willie sprang to open the restaurant door and then leaned out and watched the couple as they walked along the waterfront and turned in at the police station.

"She's gone home with him," he announced to the assembled diners. The locals grinned, except for a visitor, a heavyset man who was dining with a girl who was not his wife, who felt uneasy at this sign of village gossip.

Hamish switched on the light in the kitchen. "This is cosy," said Sarah, taking off her jacket.

The kitchen was gleaming and the wood stove was burning merrily. All the dishes had been washed. A note lay on the table. Hamish picked it up and read it. "Have fun, Angela." He crumpled it quickly in his hand and stuffed it into his pocket.

"I'll make us some coffee and then take you through to the computer. Milk and sugar?"

"Just black, please."

He made two mugs of coffee and then led her through to the police office. She sat down in front of the computer. "I think you'd better go away and read a book or something, Hamish. This might take some time."

"There's nothing I can do?"

"Nothing but wait and pray."

Hamish went through to his living room. Angela had cleared all the dead ash out of the fireplace and set it ready to light. He put a match to it and sat down in front of the crackling blaze. He then rose and switched on the television set. An alternative comedian was telling bad jokes. Alternative in Hamish's mind meant humourless. He switched the channel. On BBC2 was a wildlife programme and he knew some creature was going to rend and destroy some other creature before the end of it. He switched again. There was a Victorian drama running which he knew would probably mean explicit sex under the corsets. There must have been a good few families in Victorian times who led blameless lives, but not according to television. The last channel available was showing a buddy-buddy, black cop, white cop bonding movie. Hamish settled back happily to watch fictional mayhem in the streets of Los Angeles.

Gradually his eyes began to close and then he plunged down into a deep, dark dream where he was in the dentist's chair and Gilchrist was leaning over him brandishing the drill. "This won't hurt," said Gilchrist, shaking his shoulder.

Hamish awoke with a start to find that it was Sarah who was shaking him by the shoulder, holding a sheaf of paper.

"Success!" she said. "I just printed out everything I thought you might want."

Hamish rubbed his eyes and sat up straight. "This is marvellous," he said, blinking at the sheaf of papers.

"The pathologist's report is on top," said Sarah proudly.

Hamish rose and switched off the television and then looked in amazement at the clock. "I am sorry, lassie. It's gone two in the morning."

"I can sleep late tomorrow. Read the pathologist's report first."

Hamish sat down again and began to read carefully. "There iss the thing," he said at last. "Nicotine poisoning, and the man didn't smoke. He was hoisted into the chair and his teeth drilled after death. My! I don't know a thing about nicotine poisoning."

"I believe you can get enough nicotine out of three cigars if you have the right equipment," said Sarah, sinking into an armchair. "I remember we did an experiment in the lab at school. The teacher wanted us to see how much gunk came out of a single cigarette."

"Maggie Bane was a physics student."

"Doesn't mean she was a chemistry student."

"But surely it's the same sort of thing."

"Not really," said Sarah. "I had a friend who was brilliant at physics at school but who nearly failed his chemistry exams."

"It would need to be someone then with access to lab equipment."

"I don't know if it would be that difficult. Any school lab equipment would do. Something like a still would do as well."

"A still! I'm sure there's plenty o' illegal stills about the Highlands. In fact, I've an idea how I can find out where one is. Can I run you back to the hotel and then I'll sit up and go through these. How did you get to the restaurant?"

"I walked."

Hamish looked at her high heels. "It's quite a way. I should have collected you. I wasnae thinking straight. How did you manage to break into the main police computer?"

She grinned. "Trade secret."

He grinned back, liking her immensely, but too excited about the papers in his hand to indulge in any more carnal thoughts.

He drove her back through the night to the Tommel Castle Hotel.

"He's at it again," said Nessie Currie to her sister as she let the curtain fall back into place.

"Who? Who?" demanded her sister, Jessie, from the darkness of the double bed.

"You sound like an owl," said Nessie. "That Hamish Macbeth, that's who it was, driving that lassie who's staying at the Tommel Castle."

"Priscilla was too good for him, too good for him. He's a philanderer. Poor Priscilla, poor Priscilla."

Sarah got down from the police Land Rover, went round to the driver's side and standing on tiptoe, kissed Hamish on the cheek through the open window.

"Will I see you tomorrow?"

"I'll be out and about on my rounds," said Hamish. "I'd like to talk to you about what I've read. I'll call you around lunchtime."

He waved and drove back to the police station and then settled down to read all the statements.

Jeannie Gilchrist, the dentist's ex-wife, had told the CID pretty much what she had told him. Mrs. Harrison's statement seemed even madder than anything she had said to him. Now to Maggie Bane. His eyes widened. There was nothing in her statement to say that she ever had any relationship with Gilchrist. Surely she knew that in the Highlands very little could be kept secret. And if the police found out she had actually been having an affair with Gilchrist, they would suspect her even more. Mrs. Albert, the woman who had come with her small son, Jamie, just after Hamish had found the body, stated that she had never been to Gilchrist before. She'd heard some stories that he'd "mucked-up" people's teeth, but she hadn't the time or money to go traipsing to Strathbane or Inverness and Gilchrist was cheap.

Other patients interviewed said pretty much the same thing. They had been suddenly hit, like Hamish, with blinding toothache and all they could think of was getting to the nearest and cheapest dentist. People sometimes said, "I wonder what Britain was like in the thirties or forties?" Try the Highlands of Scotland, thought Hamish. Bad teeth, stodgy food and the last corner of Britain where's women's lib had not found a foothold. He remembered the wife of a crofter who rose early to clean the rooms at a hotel and then to serve the breakfasts. When she returned to the croft, she had to help with the lambing. In the evening she returned to the hotel to serve the dinners, and one night when she returned home at midnight, she had said to her husband, who was lying on the hearth rug in front of the fire, "I think I'd better see the doctor, Angus. I'm that tired these days." "Och, woman," said Angus, "I'll tell ye what's up with ye. Ye're chust damn lazy." And the crofter's wife had laughed with pride and admiration, saying, "That's men for you."

He flipped over the pages. Ah, here it was. One of the townspeople, a Mrs. Reekie. "Mr. Gilchrist was romancing that Maggie Bane. I seen them with my own eyes, going into her house, night after night and not driving off till the morning either."

That statement had been taken by Detective Harry Mac-Nab, not long after Hamish had seen Maggie Bane. Blair would read that and have the receptionist picked up again and taken to Strathbane for another grilling.

But what was missing from all the statements, from townspeople, from patients, was the necessary hatred. Had it not been that a great deal of strength had been required, then Maggie Bane would certainly be the number one suspect in his book. Unless she had an accomplice. There was that mysterious hour she had taken off to go shopping. There was surely something she had not been telling the police apart from her affair with Gilchrist. Or if she had nothing to do with the murder, had Gilchrist been expecting someone, someone he had not wanted her to see or hear?

He returned to the pathologist's report. The nicotine had been put in the coffee. The pathologist seemed sure of that. Again back to Maggie Bane.

He picked up her statement. She had made him a cup of coffee as usual and taken it in. He had not drunk it when she was present. She had put it over on the desk by the window and then had left. But she knew, thought Hamish, about all that sugar Gilchrist took in his coffee, sugar that would kill the taste of any poison.

Back to the other statements. Mrs. Macbean. The woman's bad temper seemed to leap off the page. She had been going to Gilchrist for two years now. She had always had trouble with her teeth. Better to get them out.

The day before the murder had been her daughter, Darleen's, first visit. No, she had never met Gilchrist outside the surgery.

Hamish rubbed his hand wearily over his eyes. His elation at getting his hands on the pathologist's report and the other statements was waning fast. He seemed to be in more of a muddle than ever. One thing at a time, he thought, putting the paper aside. A night's sleep and then start to ask about stills.

In the morning, he decided to take a walk up the hill to visit the seer, Angus Macdonald. Whether old Angus actually had the gift of the second sight, Hamish doubted very much. But Angus maintained his reputation by picking up every bit of gossip in the Highlands that he could.

There was an arctic wind blowing in from the east. The tops of the mountains were covered with snow and a metallic smell on the wind heralded more snow to come. The seer's cottage was on top of a hill with a path winding up to the front door. It looked rather like the illustration in a children's book.

Angus opened the door as Hamish approached. Angus looked more like one of the minor prophets than ever with his long grey hair and long grey beard.

"I knew you would be needing my help," he said simply. "Come ben."

His light eyes raked Hamish up and down, looking for the expected present, before he turned away. People usually brought the seer something, a bottle of whisky or a homemade cake. Only Hamish Macbeth did not usually bother.

"Well, Hamish, sit yourself down," said the seer, swinging the blackened kettle on its chain over the peat fire.

"Now, then," he went on, a flicker of malice in his eyes, "romance hass come back into the life of our Hamish Macbeth. But I see no hope, no hope at all, laddie."

"I am not interested in my love life at the moment, Angus," said Hamish stiffly. "Thon dentist was murdered with a dose of nicotine poison. Now the nicotine could have been extracted from cigarettes or probably cigars in a still. Who's running a still around Braikie?"

"Aye, we'll have our tea first. I am a poor man, Hamish, and that farm salmon I get in the supermarket iss not a patch on the wild ones. It seems this age since I've had a salmon out of the river."

"You old moocher," said Hamish crossly.

"Och, it takes one to know one."

"All right. I'll get you a salmon."

"When?"

"This night. I'll bring it along tomorrow."

"Good lad." Angus swung the now boiling kettle off the fire. He filled a teapot, then two mugs.

"Let me see," he crooned, settling back in his chair. "You want to know about an illegal still. I would not want the honest to be arrested."

"Running a still is dishonest and you know it, Angus. Chust tell me who it is and I'll ask a few questions and if they're not involved in the murder, I won't be taking the matter further." Unless they're producing stuff that might turn the population blind, thought Hamish.

Angus closed his eyes. "I will chust be consulting the spirit world."

Hamish suppressed an exclamation of impatience.

"Aye, I see twa men. There's a wee white house which looks like the Smiley brothers' croft."

"Stourie and Pete Smiley?" demanded Hamish sharply.

Angus opened his eyes and gazed at Hamish reproachfully. "You've frightened the spirits away."

"Oh, really, were they illegal spirits?"

"The spirits do not like levity. Och, well, I shouldnae be too hard on you, Hamish. Thon pretty lassie at the Tommel Castle Hotel iss going to cause you the pain and grief."

"You know what I think," said Hamish. "I think you forecast doom and gloom and that's all people remember about your predictions and if you go on forecasting doom and gloom the whole damn time, then some of it iss bound to come true."

"You're chust cross because you know you've got to keep your promise and get me that salmon."

Hamish drained his mug and walked to the door. He nodded to the seer, who grinned maliciously at him from his chair by the fire.

"All your predictions are based on gossip, Angus. What have you heard about the girl at Tommel Castle Hotel?"

"I only hear the voices in my head, Hamish, and they tell me she's not for you."

Hamish made an exclamation of disgust and strode out and walked down the hill. Forget Sarah. He had what he wanted. An illegal still at Braikie. Now if he told Blair, the equivalent of a SWAT team would descend on the Smiley brothers and take their croft apart. But they would arrive with such noise and fuss that before they even got there, the Highland tom-toms would have been beating and by the time they arrived, there would be no trace of a still.

He was also anxious to confront Maggie Bane, but he had heard she was back at police headquarters.

He walked back to the police station to collect the Land Rover.

Jimmy Anderson was lounging outside.

"How are the investigations going, Hamish?"

"As well as a local policeman can investigate while being kept in the dark about everything."

"Well, there's a fuss at Strathbane. Last night some hacker broke into the police computer records."

"And why aren't you somewhere looking for the hacker?"

Jimmy grinned evilly.

He put an arm around Hamish's shoulders. "Shall we be having a wee look inside? Yes, I'm looking for the hacker.

"Why do you think I'm here?"

CHAPTER FIVE

*It requires a surgical operation to get a joke well
into a Scotch understanding.*

—Rev. Sydney Smith

Hamish's mind worked furiously. How could they have found
out? If only he knew more about computers other than the
basic word processing necessary for filing reports.

"Can I use your toilet afore I take ye apart?" said Jimmy.

"Aye, go ahead, the bathroom's through there."

Jimmy went into the bathroom, Hamish ran into the police
office, seized up the pile of printouts and stuffed them up
under his dark blue uniform sweater. The phone rang.

"Hamish?" said Sarah's voice.

The flush went in the bathroom.

"Sarah," said Hamish urgently. "They've found out they've
been hacked into and suspect me."

"They can't know exactly."

"Why? How? What do I do?"

"Stick to your guns and look innocent."

Jimmy walked into the police office.

"I will be looking into that matter right away, madam," said Hamish.

"Call me later," Sarah said and hung up.

Hamish turned to face Jimmy. "I'm flattered you think I should have enough expertise to hack into any computer."

"You're a clever bastard, Hamish. Someone hacked into Blair's records during the night and it wisnae Blair."

"Look around for a computer buff, Jimmy, but don't come bothering me. Blair's off his trolley. You know what he's like. One sniff of trouble and he decides it must be coming from me."

Jimmy sat down behind the desk and opened the bottom drawer. "Where's the whisky?"

"I don't think I should tell you," said Hamish crossly. "You chust go back and tell Blair to spend his time looking for criminals instead of bothering innocent policemen."

"Don't be so sour. It was a way of getting away from the big grump."

"All right. You can have a dram and then off with you."

Hamish went through to the kitchen and found a bottle in the cupboard with the groceries. He collected a glass and then walked back through to join Jimmy.

"Great, man, pour it out."

"You'll be getting as much o' a problem wi' the booze as Blair," commented Hamish, pouring a measure of whisky into the glass.

"Not me. I can take it or leave it. The only problem I've got wi' booze these days is that I don't get nearly enough o' it."

"So what's Blair doing about this mysterious hacker apart from wasting time sending you over here to annoy me and drink my Scotch?"

"He says someone found out his password and he never told anyone what it was."

"Probably told someone in a bar at the top of his voice. What was the password? I assume he's changed it."

"Crap."

"No, seriously, Jimmy, what was the password?"

"I'm telling you. Clean your ears. The password was CRAP."

And how did a nicely brought up lady like Sarah think of that, marvelled Hamish.

"So what's new?" he asked aloud.

"Maggie Bane was having an affair wi' Gilchrist and so when she said she wasn't, she was lying in her teeth, so it stands to reason that she was lying about everything else. She says she didn't want to lose her good name. Can you believe it? Like a Victorian novel. But, by God, she sticks to everything else and Blair howled and howled, but he couldnae move her."

"So who else is there? And what did Gilchrist die of?"

"Nicotine poison."

"Now there's a thing. And the man didnae smoke."

"How did you know that?"

"There were no cigarettes or ashtrays anywhere and a big NO SMOKING sign on the surgery wall."

"Come on, Hamish. Every doctor and dentist has a NO SMOKING sign up these days."

"But he had two posters in the reception about the evils of smoking. A smoker wouldn't have put them up."

"Far-fetched to me. Maggie Bane could have put them up."

"But she didn't. She smokes herself."

"So she says. Oh, well, nobody saw Gilchrist puff a cigarette and anyway, even if he had, it wouldn't have given him nicotine poisoning enough to kill him like that."

"So who's the favourite suspect apart from Maggie?"

"Blessed if I know."

"And what about thon burglary?"

"Johnny King had done time for two counts of drunken driving."

"Time?" Hamish looked puzzled. "I thought they would just take his license away."

"The second time was when he drove into the front of a police station. Peter Sampson has no record. Family boy. Clean living."

"And what of Macbean?"

"Now let me think. Any more whisky?"

Hamish sighed and pushed the bottle across to him.

Jimmy poured a generous measure, sat back in his chair and put his feet on the desk.

"Macbean's never been in trouble. I mean, he's never been arrested. He was running a hotel in Selkirk for a long time and then suddenly got fired. Owners just say that the profits were going down and down but they admitted that they could not pin anything on Macbean."

"And Mrs. Macbean?"

"Nothing there. Born Agnes Macwhirter. Born in Leith. Married Macbean twenty-five years ago. Nasty bit of work. Always in a temper about something."

"Any reports of her husband beating her up?"

"No, but I hope he does and regularly. If I was married to that one, I'd beat her up myself."

"I heard on the grapevine that Gilchrist and Maggie Bane had a bit o' a scene in a pub in Inverness. If they broke up, it stands to reason that there might be a new woman on the scene."

"If there was," said Jimmy, "something'll come up sooner or later."

"Then there's the ex," said Hamish, thinking aloud. "She was married to him. She seems a nice woman but you can never tell from the outside, can you? She might have hated him like poison."

"She's got clear of him so she had nae reason to bump him off."

Hamish picked up the whisky bottle and replaced the top. "I don't want to keep you, Jimmy. I've got the work to do."

"Oh, aye, forgot to feed the hens, did you?"

When Hamish had finally seen a reluctant Jimmy on his way, he ran into the police office, seized the phone and dialled the Tommel Castle Hotel and asked for Sarah.

When she came on the line, he asked, "How did you guess Blair's password?"

Her voice sounded amused. "I maintain there are about twenty variations on passwords. From what you told me about Blair, I was sure it would be some sort of swear word. Is everything all right? They will know someone used Blair's password, but if he has trouble with drink, then he'll begin to wonder who he actually told and he won't be able to remember. I wouldn't worry about it. What are you doing now?"

"I'm going to interview a couple of people. Do you feel like doing some amateur investigation?"

"You want me to come with you?"

"No, I wondered if you would like to go over to The Scotsman Hotel today and listen to what's going on. They won't talk if they see me, but they might not guard their mouths in front of a tourist."

"Good. I'd like to do that."

Hamish gripped the receiver hard. "And maybe we could meet up later? I could pick you up."

"Seven o'clock will be fine, if you're through by then."

"That's chust grand . . . grand. I'll see you then. Bye."

Hamish put down the receiver and stood for a moment smiling idiotically at the phone. Then he pulled himself together and decided it was time he visited the Smiley brothers.

Small fine pellets of snow were beginning to be whipped down the loch on an icy wind. He gave a little sigh. Then he thought of Sarah. He hoped the snow would not get worse. He did not want to think of her skidding into a ditch on the Lairg road. But ahead of him loomed a large yellow truck. The Sutherland road gritters were already on the job. He passed the truck and headed off into the thickening snow. By the time he reached the Smiley brothers' croft, the snow had suddenly stopped and pale yellow sunlight was flooding the whitened fields and the low croft house.

He noticed there was a new extension at the back of the croft house: a long low building with a corrugated iron roof and with steel shutters over all the windows.

He was just getting out of the Land Rover when the door of the cottage opened and Stourie Smiley came out to meet him, followed by his brother, Pete. Hamish knew both of them slightly, but he was taken aback again by their appearance. They looked living proof that trolls still walked the earth. Both were squat and barrel-chested and hairy. Thick mats of hair covered both their heads, and hair sprouted on their cheekbones, and tufts of hair poked out of their ears. Both had small, gleaming wet eyes and red faces. Both had very long arms.

"It's yoursel', Macbeth," said Stourie. "What brings ye? Ye've got the sheep dip papers." A visit by the police to a croft in the Highlands did not usually mean a report of death or accident, but merely a demand for sheep dip papers.

"Can we go inside and sit down for a minute?" asked Hamish. "I need your help."

"Okay," said Pete, "but don't take too lang ower it. We've got work to do."

He led the way into the croft house kitchen, a bleak stone-flagged room with a plastic-covered table in the centre and a few hard upright chairs.

Hamish sat down, took off his cap and put it on the table. "It is my belief you are running an illegal still."

"Whit?" demanded Stourie. "Who tellt you that?"

The two trolls bristled at Hamish and the cold air of the kitchen was suddenly full of menace.

"Before you get your lies ready," said Hamish, "listen to me. Thon dentist, Gilchrist, was poisoned with nicotine. Anyone who had a still could have extracted the nicotine by means of a still. Now, either you cooperate or I'll get a team over from Strathbane with a search warrant and right behind them will come the Customs and Excise. If you give me a dram of your stuff and I consider it safe and not liable to kill anyone, I'll not be booking you. But I need to know if either of you had a grudge against Gilchrist, and then since I'm pretty sure you know your competitors, I'll need some names."

They looked at him in truculent silence and then Pete's small wet eyes travelled past Hamish to the fireplace. Hamish swung round. A shotgun was hanging on the wall.

"Don't even think of it, man," he said. "That's another breach of the law. That gun should be locked in a gun cabinet. You have one. Sergeant Macgregor over at Cnothan reported you had one."

"Aye, well, we'd rather deal wi' Macgregor than you." Stourie looked surly.

Had Macgregor really checked, wondered Hamish.

"So let's not take all day about this," he said. "Did either of you go to Gilchrist?"

Pete suddenly grinned and so did Stourie. Hamish blinked. Both men were toothless. Pete jerked his head in the direction of the sink. Hamish looked across. There were two tumblers of water by the sink and in each tumbler resided a pair of false teeth, the dentures grotesquely imitating the grins across the table from him.

"We both had all our teeth out in our twenties," said Stourie. "We don't need no dentists."

"So you didn't know Gilchrist?"

"Didnae even know what the man looked like."

"That's strange, you pair being so near Braikie. It's a small town. Surely someone pointed the man out to you."

Stourie spat contemptuously on the floor. "We don't talk to them in Braikie."

"So who else has a still?"

"We arenae saying we hae one," said Stourie, "but I guess you could say if we had, we wouldnae want any competition."

"Meaning you're the only ones you know about?"

They looked at him in sullen silence.

"All right, I'll leave it there at the moment. Give me a dram."

They looked at each other and then Stourie gave a little nod. Pete went over and opened a kitchen cupboard and took down a bottle of whisky, tipped one set of false teeth out into the sink and poured the whisky into the glass.

Oh, well, thought Hamish, the alcohol will probably act as a disinfectant.

He sampled the whisky and then raised his eyebrows. It was pretty good, quite smooth, not as good as a regular legal blend, but certainly not likely to poison anyone. Hamish had a good palate for whisky and knew that they had not given him Johnnie Walker or something like that to pass off as their own.

"I'll be on my way." He got to his feet. "That's a big extension ye've built onto the cottage."

"Lambing shed," said Stourie laconically.

"Well, now, the poor wee things must grow up fair blind in the dark," said Hamish sarcastically. "The windows are all shuttered."

"We aye take the shutters off when we're lambing," jeered Pete. "As a crofter yourself, you should hae guessed that."

"Now, listen here." Hamish Macbeth turned in the doorway. "I'm turning a blind eye to your practises but only for the moment. I'll give you a couple of months to pack up. If I hear by then that you're still making whisky, I'll report you."

"It iss no wunner you became a policeman, Macbeth," said Stourie viciously, "because without that uniform, you'd chust be a lang drip o' nothing."

Hamish put his cap firmly on his flaming red hair. "Behave yourselves," he snapped and went out into the cold day.

It was clouding over again and a few snowflakes were beginning to drift down. Against the black clouds massing to the west curved a glorious rainbow. He stood looking at it, a half smile on his lips, and then he clutched his head and let out a groan as pain stabbed over his left temple. Hamish could not remember when he last had a headache. Could it have been that whisky?

But he belonged to the school of thought which firmly believes that if you pay no attention to physical ailments, they go away. He drove into Braikie and parked in the main street. The pain was now nagging and persistent. He found he was outside a chemist's shop. He went in and walked through the racks of cosmetics and vitamin pills to the pharmacy counter.

Behind the counter was a plump little girl in her early twenties. Her buxom figure was covered in a tight white coat. She had a piggy little face and a turned-up nose. Hamish had often read that a turned-up nose was supposed to be saucy and attractive. He had never found it so. But he had to admit that despite his headache, he was well aware that this buxom piggy little blonde was exuding a strong air of sexuality, so strong it hung in the air like musk.

"I've got a bad headache," he said. "Can you give me something?"

"The best thing is aspirin," she said.

"What about one of those extra-strength painkillers?"

"Just a rip-off," she said cheerfully. "Aspirin's cheaper and does the job the same. You smell of whisky. Maybe you shouldn't drink so early in the day."

"I was out at the Smiley brothers on a case," said Hamish stiffly, not liking the implication that he was a drunk.

"Oh, another one of those headaches. It'll go away all by itself the minute you have another dram."

Hamish looked at her curiously and she gave him a cheeky wink. Apart from himself the shop was empty of customers. He leaned forward on the counter. "So you know that the Smiley brothers operate a still?"

"I don't want to get them into trouble, but, yes, everyone knows it."

I'm slipping, thought Hamish. And I forgot Angus's salmon.

"The pharmacist, Mr. Cody, says there's migraine and there's tension headaches and there's the headache from the Smileys' hooch. You don't need aspirin. You need another drink. Works a treat."

Despite the pain in his head, Hamish smiled. The shop door opened and a small, fussy man came in. "Everything all right, Kylie?" he asked. When she nodded, he said, "You can take a break."

He went through into the back.

"Come and have a drink with me," said Hamish.

"Righty-ho. Just get my coat."

She emerged a few moments later wearing a scarlet wool coat over a thin yellow blouse, tight short jersey skirt and heels so high that Hamish thought she must be very tiny indeed when she took them off, for as they walked in the direction of the pub, she hardly came up to his shoulder.

"What are you having?" he asked when they entered the smoky, dreary barroom of The Drouthy Crofter.

"Same as you. Straight whisky. And make it a couple of doubles."

He went to the bar, collected their order and carried the glasses over to a corner table where Kylie was already seated.

She shrugged off her coat. The yellow blouse had a deep V revealing that Kylie had the sort of cleavage only usually seen in the magazines on the top shelf of the newsagents. He dragged his gaze from it and raised his glass. "Let's hope this works."

And it did, almost immediately. He blinked at her in relief. "Do you always join customers for a drink?"

She giggled. "Only the sexy ones."

He was not surprised that despite the fact that the Smileys' still was obviously pretty well known that no one had come forward to report it. There are some things in the Highlands which would be regarded as crimes anywhere else in Britain that people here regarded as quite respectable. Poaching, provided it was the occasional salmon or deer, was not regarded as illegal. It was every Highlander's birthright to take a deer from the hill and a fish from the river, no matter who owned the land. And a whisky still was regarded as about as innocent as making home-made cakes.

But as he surveyed sexy little Kylie, he began to wonder if Gilchrist had ever made a play for her. How Gilchrist had been able to attract such a beautiful young girl as Maggie Bane was beyond him. But he had, and so it followed that other women might have found him attractive—young women.

"I'm investigating the murder of the dentist," he said.

"Oh, him." She shrugged. "I don't understand anyone going to that man. I went there once. I knew all I needed was a simple little filling, but he says it had to come out. No thank you, I said, and got the hell out of there."

"So that was the only time you saw him?"

"You're looking a me as if I'm the first murderer. Why on earth suspect me?"

"I don't suspect you. You're a very pretty girl and Gilchrist liked the ladies."

"I had nothing to do with him." But that sexy aura had disappeared. It had been turned off somewhere deep inside her. Her eyes roved restlessly around the bar. "Headache better?"

"Yes, thank you."

"Well, if you don't mind, I see some of my friends over there."

And without waiting for his reply, she got to her feet and went over to join a group of men at the bar.

I'd better ask around about that one, thought Hamish. She was all right until I started asking about Gilchrist.

He left the pub and walked back towards where he had parked the Land Rover. He saw he was passing a fishmongers and stopped. "Special Offer. Fresh Salmon." The sign in the window caught his eye. Salmon was selling for £1.80 a pound. He decided it would be worth buying one for the seer. He was sure the salmon was farmed rather than wild, but he was equally sure that old Angus would not be able to tell the difference.

He went in and bought a ten-pound salmon, big enough for that old leech, he thought crossly.

He took the salmon back to the police station and threw away the fishmonger's bag, wrapped it in kitchen foil, and drove this time up to the seer's.

He laid the salmon on the table in front of the seer. Angus studied it curiously after he had taken it out of its foil wrapper. Then he went off without a word into the nether regions and came back carrying a small stone on the end of a cord.

"What's that?" asked Hamish. "Your pet rock?"

"Aye jeering at things you do not understand, Hamish. This iss my crystal."

He waved it over the salmon. The "crystal" swung round over the fish like a pendulum.

"This iss the farm salmon, Hamish."

"It is not!"

"Aye, the pendulum sees it all. You forgot last night and it's cauld the day and so you thought you could pass a shop-bought fish on poor Angus."

"Havers." Hamish wrapped up the salmon. "I'll have it myself."

"If I were you, Hamish Macbeth, I waud be thinking of getting Angus the real thing tonight or something bad will happen to ye."

"You mean you'll put a curse on me?"

"Don't sneer. There are mair things in heaven and earth . . ."

"Horatio."

"Who's he?"

"Never mind. I'm out of here."

Hamish drove off. What could the old phony do to him? He was damned if he was going to take his rod out on the river in this weather.

The wind had dropped and large Christmas card flakes of snow were spiralling down from a leaden sky. He went home and made himself a scrap lunch, that is he ate tuna out of the can with a fork while leaning against the kitchen counter. Then he set out for Braikie again. He nodded to the policeman who stood on guard outside the dentist's building and then went on up the stairs to the top landing and knocked on Fred Sutherland's door.

The old man answered his knock promptly and said, "You better come in."

Hamish followed him in and sat down. "I want to ask you about the murder."

"My, my. That was a thing. Poisoned him and drilled all his teeth. My, my."

"How did you hear all that? The method of killing was not in the papers."

"This is a small town. Everyone gets to hear everything."

"That's why I'm here. There's this young lassie works for the chemist. Kylie something."

"Kylie Fraser. Thon's a cheeky wee thing. Called me old man. Cheek!"

"You wouldn't have happened to hear if she had been seen at any time in the company of Gilchrist?"

"He was old enough to hae been her faither."

"True. But that hadn't seemed to have stopped him chasing young ladies."

"There's a lot o' talk about her. She's aye in the pub wi' the fellows. But I never heard o' her being wi' Gilchrist."

"Could you let me know if you hear anything?"

"Aye, I'll do that. I'm a regular at the Old Timers Club at the community hall. The biddies that go there hear every blessed thing."

"Thanks, Mr. Sutherland. And I would be grateful if you would be discreet about it."

Fred laid a gnarled finger alongside his nose and winked. "Dinnae fash yourself. I'll let you know."

Hamish then ran lightly down the stairs and went into the dress shop. As usual it was empty of customers. The yellow cellophane was still across the windows casting a jaundiced light around the interior. Mrs. Edwardson came forward to meet him.

"I remember you," she said, peering up at him. "You discovered the body. Have you any idea who did it?"

"No, that I haven't, Mrs. Edwardson. You see, no one seems to give me any idea of what Gilchrist was like as a man."

"I knew him a little bit. He fancied himself with the ladies. Smooth. Unctuous, is the word. Smarmy. Surely there are papers and letters and photographs at his home that might give you an idea?"

Hamish had already thought of that but did not want to lower his position on the case in her eyes by telling her that the CID were covering that. He frowned suddenly. There must be some report in the files now of the contents of Gilchrist's home. He wondered if Sarah could access those, or if that was taking too great a risk.

"What do you know of Kylie Fraser?"

"The tarty little piece of baggage that's works for the chemist?"

"Her, yes."

"Apart from the fact that she's getting herself the reputation of a tart and a lush, no."

"Would Gilchrist have made a pass at her?"

"He might have done. But the fact is I don't go out much." Her face was sad. "At the end of the day I feel so tired, I usually sit down in front of the television set and fall asleep."

"If you hear anything let me know."

"I most certainly will."

"Just to remind you, my name is Hamish Macbeth and I am the policeman over at Lochdubh."

"Yes, I know that."

He hesitated. He had been about to caution her to be discreet. Then he thought, it might be interesting if Kylie found out he was asking questions about her. He thanked Mrs. Edwardson and left the shop and stood for a moment outside in the snow. Then he set off in the direction of the pub. Time to ask more questions and hope his interest in her got back to Kylie.

The Drouthy Crofter was fairly quiet apart from a juke box blaring in the corner. Hamish went up to the bar. The barman eyed his uniform suspiciously. "I would like to ask you a few questions about one of your customers, Kylie Fraser."

"Oh, thon wee lassie? What's she been up to?"

"I just wondered if she had ever been in here with Gilchrist, the dentist who was murdered?"

"Naw. She hangs about with the young lads. She's good fun."

"Ever get drunk and disorderly?"

"Och, you know the young folk. They usually drink that alcoholic lemonade and get a bit pissed and noisy. Mind you, Kylie always drinks straight whisky. They all live locally and don't drive here, so it's not as if I have to worry."

"Let me know if you hear anything."

Later that day Kylie stood with her friend, Tootsie Duffy, outside Mrs. Edwardson's shop. Mrs. Edwardson was just locking up. "Did you ever see such fashions?" crowed Kylie. "I wouldnae be seen dead in one of them. Tell you what, one o' them would make a good shroud."

Tootsie shrieked with mirthless laughter. Tootsie hardly ever found anything funny but she supplied a sort of canned laughter to her friend's sallies.

Mrs. Edwardson whipped round and stared at Kylie with contempt. "You'd better just watch yourself, my girl. The police have been asking me about you and Gilchrist."

Kylie stood, her small mouth hanging a little open. "What d'you mean?"

"Just what I said." Mrs. Edwardson stalked off, her back rigid.

Tootsie moved a wad of gum to the other side of her mouth and asked, "You and auld Gilchrist?"

"Spiteful old twat," said Kylie viciously. "I could do with a drink."

They walked into The Drouthy Crofter, both teetering on high heels, oblivious to already cold and wet feet. Tootsie's long skinny legs were purple with cold. But one must suffer to be beautiful.

Kylie pouted when she saw the pub was still empty. She did not like spending her own money.

"Getting yourself in trouble with the police?" asked the barman after he had taken their order.

"What is this?" demanded Kylie angrily.

"That tall policeman wi' the red hair was in here asking if Gilchrist had been getting his leg over."

"It's police harassment," said Tootsie. "You should report him, Kylie."

Kylie tossed her short blonde locks. "And I will, too," she said savagely. "Just you see if I don't."

Sarah sat in a corner of the bar-reception area at The Scotsman Hotel, pretending to read a book, but listening carefully. Two men who looked like detectives went into the hotel office. Then a small angry-looking middle-aged woman went up to the bar and said, "Give me a whisky. The decent stuff."

Sarah looked at her curiously as the barman said, "Right you are, Mrs. Macbean."

Mrs. Macbean had a headful of bright green plastic rollers. Mrs. Macbean picked up her drink and turned around. She saw Sarah looking at her and glared. Sarah smiled tentatively.

Mrs. Macbean walked over. "Were you looking at me?"

Sarah smiled into her truculent face. "I'm just a tourist and I wanted to ask someone if this hotel was a comfortable place to stay."

The anger left Mrs. Macbean's face and she sat down opposite Sarah. "I'm married to the manager," she said. "The rooms are clean and the rates are cheap. Then we have the bingo Saturday night, if you're interested."

"Not really," said Sarah. "I never win anything. I am one of life's losers."

"Me too." Mrs. Macbean took a moody sip at her whisky. "Men," she said bitterly.

"Tell me about it. They're all bastards," said Sarah encouragingly. "We're still brought up to think the knight on the white charger is coming to look after us."

"But all we get is horse shit," said Mrs. Macbean. She jerked her thumb in the direction of the office. "That's all he talks."

Normally Sarah would quickly have disengaged herself from such a conversation.

"My husband's the same," she said.

"You don't wear a wedding ring."

Sarah gave her a slow smile. "I threw it down the toilet, and do you know why?"

"Go on. Tell me." Mrs. Macbean now looked positively friendly.

"He beat me up."

"And you took it?"

Sarah spread her hands in a deprecatory gesture. "What else could I do? He was stronger than me. So I got a divorce."

"Lassie, lassie." Mrs. Macbean shook her head and a curler fell into her glass of whisky. "Don't you see that's what they want? You get a divorce and settle for lousy terms or nothing at all. A man isnae as strong as a woman with a breadknife in her hand, remember that."

Sarah looked at her, wide-eyed. "You sound to me like a very brave woman."

Mrs. Macbean took another sip of whisky. Sarah noticed with horror that she was straining it through the roller, which had floated to the top of her glass, but did not want to say anything for fear of drying up this interesting conversation.

Mrs. Macbean preened. "You have to learn to take care of yourself. Brian, that's him." She jerked a thumb again in the direction of the office. "He used his fists on me last week. Well, he likes hot chocolate in the mornings so I put a whole lot of laxative in it. 'You lay a hand on me and next time it'll be poison, buster,' that's what I said."

Sarah gazed at her in well-feigned admiration.

"He's useless, that's what he is. Did you know we had the burglary here?"

"No!"

"Fact. Two hundred and fifty thousands pounds out o' the safe."

"How? Gelignite?"

"Naw. The damn fool had this safe wi' a wooden back. Thought no one would find out."

"But he'll get the insurance."

"I don't think so. The insurance company said a safe like that was jist like leaving the money lying on the bar."

"How terrible for you. And I'll bet he made you think it was all your fault."

"That's it. That's what he did."

"But he couldn't get away with it. I mean, you didn't buy the safe."

"Isn't that what I told him? He said I musta told someone about the wooden back on the safe. As if I would!"

Sarah's fine eyes glowed with sympathy. "I think you have a very hard life, Mrs. Macbean."

Mrs. Macbean took another roller-flavoured sip of whisky. "Aye, that's the truth."

"I never thought of any crime being committed up here," said Sarah. "I mean, people like me come up here for the quality of life."

"Quality of life! Ha! Sheep and rain and cold and a lot o' stupid teuchters."

"Teuchters?"

"Highlanders. Sly, malicious and stupid. I hate the bastards."

Sarah looked puzzled. "But they're all Scottish. Just like you."

"Don't insult me." Sarah covered her glass as another roller flew through the air. Mrs. Macbean leaned forward and whispered, "It's like one o' those primitive tribes up the Amazon. They havenae *evolved*."

"You are a philosopher."

"I've got my head screwed on."

"I did hear about a murder up here. Some dentist."

Mrs. Macbean's face suddenly closed up. She had a mouth like Popeye's and it seemed to disappear up under her nose.

"Got to go," she muttered.

Sarah watched her march off, and then stop at the bar to whisper something to the barman. What would Hamish make of that, she wondered. Eager to tell all the secrets of her marriage life and talk about the burglary, but clams up when Gilchrist is mentioned.

The barman approached her. "Would you be wanting anything else?" he asked truculently.

"No, thank you."

"Right." He picked up her unfinished drink and walked off with the glass.

Sarah's protest died on her lips. She felt she had done enough investigation for Hamish Macbeth for one day. Through the smeared glass of the windows, she could see the snow was falling ever thicker. She stood up and put on her coat. She had never credited herself with an overactive imagination, yet she could swear as she walked to the door that the air was heavy with menace.

CHAPTER SIX

I have no great relish for the country; it is a kind of healthy grave.

—Rev. Sydney Smith

The floodlights outside the Tommel Castle Hotel came as a relief to Sarah, who had endured a terrifying drive back from The Scotsman.

She parked the car she had borrowed from the hotel, and, bending her head, she darted through the blinding sheets of driving snow and into the warmth and security of the hotel. She went up to her room to change although she wondered if Hamish Macbeth could possibly keep their date in such weather. She smiled as she took a simple black wool dress down from a hanger in the wardrobe. She had not expected to be dressing up at all. But she could hardly continue her hiking in such weather and it was marvellous to be secure in a comfortable and warm hotel room while the storm raged outside.

At seven o'clock promptly, she was waiting at the reception desk. Mr. Johnson, the manager, came out of his office. "Will you be having dinner here tonight?"

"I should think so," replied Sarah. "Hamish was to meet me here at seven, but I don't think he'll make it. Do you usually have dreadful weather like this?"

"Not until about January, and even then, it's usually central Scotland that gets the worst of it. We're nearer to the Gulf Stream up here and that often keeps the worst of the snow away, but every few years, we get something nasty like this."

The hotel door opened and Hamish came in and stood brushing the snow from his clothes. He was wearing snowshoes.

"That's right," said Mr. Johnson sarcastically. "Leave a snow-drift on the floor."

"Good for the carpet." Hamish bent down and unstrapped his snowshoes. He was wearing a one-piece ski suit which he unzipped and stepped out of and hung on a coat rack in the corner. He was dressed in a checked shirt and dark green cor-duroy trousers. He fished in his trouser pocket and drew out a tie.

"If you're thinking of dining here, Hamish," said the man-ager, "then you don't need to bother about the tie, not on an evening like this. You'll be about the only people in the dining room. A party of ten who were supposed to be here by now are stranded down in Inverness by the bad weather."

"Right you are." Hamish stuffed the tie back in his pocket. "Are you ready to eat?" he asked Sarah.

She nodded. "I didn't have much for lunch."

They walked together into the dining room. Hamish looked around. This had been the family dining room when Tommel Castle had been a family home instead of a hotel. He could re-member the long mahogany dining table, the gleaming silver and fine china. The oriental rugs had gone and the floor was covered with serviceable fitted carpet and the room dotted with separate tables. Jenkins, once the Halburton-Smythes' butler and now the hotel's maître d', approached them and handed them menus. His face was stiff with disapproval. He loathed Hamish.

Jenkins was a snob.

"Ignore him," said Hamish. "He aye looks as if he's got a bad smell under his nose."

They ordered and then looked at each other. Hamish was struck again by Sarah's beauty and Sarah thought Hamish looked very endearing with his red hair still tousled from the storm.

"So how did you get on?" asked Hamish, privately glad that Jenkins had given their order to a humble waitress to deal with and had taken himself off, not because he was intimidated in any way by Jenkins, but because the butler reminded him of happier days when he had been so much in love with Priscilla. He gave a little sigh. He wouldn't like any of that pain back again. People babbled on about love in song and verse. Hamish thought love should come with a government health warning. Love seemed to mean a short period of rosy elation followed by months and years of dark agony and worry and tearing jealousy.

"What are you thinking about?" asked Sarah.

Hamish pulled himself together. "I was thinking of the day I've had. There's something there that I'm missing." He told her about Kylie, about the Smiley brothers, and then asked, "And how did you get on?"

Sarah carefully repeated her conversation with Mrs. Macbean, ending with, "I was glad to get out of there, Hamish. The very air had become threatening."

"That's interesting. Villainy can produce that sort of atmosphere."

"It could be. On the other hand, I got the impression that Mrs. Macbean was a bitter and unbalanced woman. I think her shrinking away from me when I mentioned Gilchrist was caused by nothing more sinister than a sort of paranoid secrecy.

Women will tell you about their private lives and then suddenly resent you bitterly for having been the recipient."

"It could be. I didn't order any wine and that sour-faced Jenkins didn't even offer us the wine menu."

"I don't feel like drinking wine. Do you?" asked Sarah.

"Not really. After that headache-inducing hooch, I don't feel like any more alcohol. Now one thing did come up today. The CID will have gone through the contents of Gilchrist's house, his papers, photographs, bankbooks, things like that. I would dearly like to know what they found out." He looked at her quizzically.

Sarah laughed. "You want me to have another go at hacking. But how on earth are we both to get to the police station in this weather?"

"Priscilla has a computer in her apartment at the top of the castle."

"Wouldn't Mr. Johnson think it odd if we asked for the key? I assume it's locked up when she is away."

"You could say she had asked you to collect something for her. I know, an address logged in her computer."

"I'll try." She stood up. "You wait here. I'll ask the manager myself."

After only a few minutes she came back and placed a key on the table. "Very trusting of him," said Sarah, sitting down. "I mean, I could be some con pretending to be a friend of Priscilla's."

"Priscilla often phones up the hotel to make sure everything is still running smoothly. That's a point. What if she phones up tonight?"

"You are friends, or so I gather. I will just tell her the truth."

"Aye, that would do." Hamish leaned back in his chair and looked at her thoughtfully. He was grateful to her, for her help, but more for her beauty and charm, which banished any wistful thoughts about the absent Priscilla. "How can you be sure you will be able to hack into the police computer this time?" he asked. "Blair will have changed his password."

"I can only try," said Sarah. She hesitated and then said, "Let me put this dinner on my bill. It's very pricey and you can't earn that much as a village policeman."

"That's kind of you, but—" He broke off as Mr. Johnson came up to them.

"Priscilla's on the phone," he said, "and you going up to her apartment to look for an address seems to be the first she's heard of it."

Hamish stood up. "Is she still on the phone?"

"Yes."

Hamish smiled at Sarah. "I'll chust be having a wee word with her."

"You can talk to her on the phone at reception," said Mr. Johnson, following him out and then standing next to him when he picked up the phone.

"Priscilla?"

"Yes, Hamish, what's all this about you and Sarah wanting the key to my apartment?"

Hamish hunched over the phone, his back to the manager.

"You've forgotten," he said. "You know you asked her to look up thon address for you."

There was a silence and then Priscilla said, "As you very well know I did nothing of the kind. You want to use my computer for something."

"Yes."

"You've got a computer at that police station."

"Aye, the weather's that bad, I don't think I'll make it back to the police station tonight."

Another silence. Somewhere behind Priscilla, a man's voice,

lazy and amused, said, "Are you going to be on that phone all night, darling?"

Hamish's heart lurched.

"Oh, go ahead," said Priscilla. "I trust Sarah even if I don't trust you, Hamish Macbeth. You obviously can't tell me about it. Phone me sometime when you can. Bye. You'd best put Johnson back on the phone and I'll tell him it's all right."

Hamish silently handed the phone back to the manager and trailed back to the dining room.

"What's the matter, Hamish?" demanded Sarah sharply. "Was she furious?"

Hamish forced a smile although his hazel eyes were bleak. "No, no, she said it wass all right. But we've got to phone her when Johnson isn't listening and tell her all about it."

"Did Priscilla help you with any of your investigations?"

"Yes, quite a few, some of them verra dangerous, too."

"You must have been very close."

"Aye, you could say that." There was an awkward silence. The shutters were down over Hamish's eyes.

"So," said Sarah brightly, "do you want coffee?"

"Yes, please."

Mr. Johnson approached them again. "Priscilla says dinner is on the house."

"That's very good of her," said Hamish, while all the time he was wondering furiously—who was that man?

After the manager had left again, Hamish wrenched his mind back to the case. "The thing about all this that bothers me is that I get this mad feeling that the burglary and the murder are connected in some way."

"I don't see how they could possibly be," remarked Sarah.

"Nor me. Chust an intuition."

Sarah privately noticed the sibilance of Hamish's Highland accent. It always seemed to become more marked when he was upset. Speaking to Priscilla had upset him. Of course it could be simply because she had ticked him off for trying to lie his way into her apartment, but that would hardly allow for the bleakness of his eyes.

"So tell me again about this still," she said aloud. "When will they appear in court?"

"They won't," said Hamish. "I've given them a warning and time to close it down."

"But what they are doing is illegal! Why didn't you arrest them?"

"There iss something in the Highlander that does not regard the illegal making of whisky as a crime," said Hamish. "Out in the Hebrides, there was a new policeman, new to the area, and he arrested two of the locals and charged them with running an illegal still. He had to take refuge on the roof of the police station as the locals tried to burn it down. There are chust some things a Highland policeman has to turn a blind eye to. Even farther south, they can get a bit vindictive.

"You've heard of the RSPB—the Royal Society for the Protection of Birds?"

"Of course. In fact, I used to be a member but I cancelled my subscription."

"Why?"

"They wrote to me appealing for funds and pointing out that they had the means to be a political force. I did not want to be associated with anything that wanted to be a political force."

"Aye, well, down in Perthshire, the gamekeepers get really tired of birds of prey and that includes golden eagles. You see, these protected birds of prey wreak havoc on stocks of young grouse and pheasant. A gamekeeper was fined £2,500 at Perth Sheriff Court after he admitted placing six hen's eggs laced with poison in an area that is home to golden eagles and other birds of prey. After that, an estate belonging to a former employee of the RSPB was vandalised. The estate has the British national collection of thousands of rare and valuable plants imported from the Himalayas. They were doused in weedkiller and "RSPB" etched in nine-foot letters on the lawn with herbicide. Although nothing could be proved, it was believed to be a revenge attack connected to the sentencing of the gamekeeper.

"Now, I am not condoning it, for it was a wicked and nasty piece of vandalism. On the other hand, there is a great deal of frustration felt among gamekeepers at the attitude of what they privately damn as a lot of moronic townees. Many in the Highlands owe their livelihood to the great shooting estates, and there's not much work anywhere else."

"It certainly feels like another part of the world up here," said Sarah, "and not like part of the British Isles at all. Sutherland. Someone told me that was the southland of the Vikings."

"I believe so," said Hamish, who in fact did not know much of Sutherland's history.

"So," said Sarah, beginning to rise, "if you've finished, let's start on a life of crime."

Hamish led the way upstairs to Priscilla's apartment. With an odd feeling, a mixture of guilt and loss, he turned the key in the lock, swung the door open and switched on the light. Everything in the living room was as cool and ordered as Priscilla herself. Sarah went straight to the computer, which sat on a desk at the window. She sat down in front of it.

"I suggest you read something, or think about something," she said over her shoulder. "This might take some time."

Hamish wandered over to the bookshelves, and suddenly conscious again of his lack of knowledge of his home county, he took down *The Sutherland Book*, edited by Donald Omand, and settled down to study it. "Sutherland," he read, "is an immense District lashed by the waves of the Minch in the west,

where the legendary blue men ride the Atlantic waves ready to lure
unwary sailors to their doom, by the cold North Sea where the
Vikings of old landed their longships, in the north-east by the fer-
tile lands of Caithness, in the south-east by the waters of the
Moray Firth, while in the south Sutherland melts into the beauty
of Ross. They are a mixed bag of Celts, Scots, Picts, Vikings, and
since the Clearances, with not an inconsiderable leavening of Low-
landers brought in to look after the sheep. Wherever they came
from, the low-lying mists, the dark lochs and tarns, the dreary
moors and the towering mountains were bound to have added to
the superstitions they already held and accentuated their fear of
the unknown."

The landscape still works on the imagination, thought
Hamish, raising his eyes from the printed page. People come up
here from the cities and begin to believe in ghosts and fairies
before they've settled for very long.

Sarah gave a little sigh. "Nothing yet?" asked Hamish.

"Not yet. Need more time."

Hamish began to read about water horses. "Of all the super-
natural creatures flitting through the pages of folklore, none
was so feared as the water horse, in Gaelic, Each Uisge. In my
own childhood, we were forbidden to go near certain lochs
which were dark and dangerous because they were said to be
the haunts of water horses. In the Highlands with stormy seas,
wave-lashed islands, short and rushing rivers and deep dark
lochs, water power was feared and looked on as malignant. This
malignancy often took the form of a horse that could change
shape into a handsome young man or even an old woman. Indeed the water horse or kelpie as it was sometimes called could
change form at will to lure its victims to their deaths."

"Got it! We're in!" cried Sarah.

He went over to join her. "Blair's new password?"

She nodded.

"What is it?"

"Shite. I thought it might be shit, but in Scotland people use the old form and say shite."

"Nasty bugger."

"Bring a chair over and we'll see if we can get a report on Gilchrist's belongings."

Hamish obediently carried a hardback chair and placed it next to her and sat down. She flicked busily through various reports and then said, "Here we go."

They eagerly read the contents of the dentist's home. He had not left a will and police were still searching for any living relative. There was no evidence of a wife before Jeannie in Inverness. There had been no photographs at all. Odd that, thought Hamish. There was a bar in the living room stocked with the finest malt whiskies. Clothes were listed as tailored and expensive, silk shirts, handmade shoes. His car was a BMW, only a few months old.

"Obviously earned a mint and spent it," murmured Hamish. "But no photographs! Passport, birth certificate, school certificates, university and dental college, but no personal records of the holiday snapshot kind. Not even a wedding photograph. Damn, this iss not helping. I wish I could see the place."

"There'll be a policeman on duty outside the place. Couldn't you just go over and chat to him and ask him if you could have a look around?"

"I could try. That's if the roads are passable in the morning."

"Will you be able to get home tonight?"

Hamish went to the window and looked out. In the hotel's floodlights, he could see white sheets of snow savagely tearing across the courtyard below.

"Might have to stay the night," he said slowly.

She looked at him. Their eyes locked. The air was suddenly charged with sexual tension. He took a half step towards her and then the door swung open and Mr. Johnson came in. "Weather's terrible, Hamish," he said. "I've arranged a wee room for you down by the office so you can stay the night. In fact, if you've finished here, I'll take you down."

"I don't know," said Hamish reluctantly. He looked hopefully at Sarah, but she was already switching off the computer. That air of sexual excitement had gone, not even a frisson.

"As a matter of fact, I am pretty tired," she said. "I'll see you in the morning, Hamish."

"Story of my life," muttered Hamish as he followed the manager downstairs.

"What?" asked Mr. Johnson.

"Nothing," said Hamish crossly. "Nothing at all."

He awoke in the morning to white stillness. The room allocated to him was one of the ones given to hotel servants. It contained the narrow bed on which he was lying, a wardrobe, chair and nothing else, not even a handbasin. He got up and went to the window. The room was on the ground floor. He looked out at a wall of white. That was all he could see. A huge drift was blocking the view.

He took his underwear off the radiator—he had washed it and put it there to dry—and then wrapped the bedcover around his nakedness, went along to the narrow bathroom used by the staff, and took a shower. By the time he was fully dressed, he could hear the scrape of shovels outside the hotel in the courtyard and the roar of tractors as the outdoor staff began to dig paths around the hotel to free the snowbound cars.

There was a smell of frying bacon. He went through to the dining room where he found Sarah eating toast and marmalade. He felt suddenly shy of her, but she smiled at him in a friendly way and said, "How are we to get anywhere today?"

"We, Sherlock?" he asked, sitting down opposite her.

"I thought that if perhaps we went to Gilchrist's house, two of us could charm our way past the policeman on duty, but I don't see how we are going to be able to move."

He looked out the long dining room windows. "It's stopped snowing, and they're better up here than they are in the cities at getting the roads cleared. As long as the snow stays off, we might be able to move. After breakfast, I'll get my snowshoes on and go back to the police station and collect the Land Rover."

"And you'll take me with you?"

"Against police regulations, but I could always explain that I found you stranded and gave you a lift. I wonder if I could ask you a favour?"

"Go on."

"Could you get back into that computer and see if there's any reference to Gilchrist's bank accounts?"

"I could, but I can tell you now, there was no reference to his finances."

Hamish banged the table in frustration. "It's aye the same," he complained. "I cannae get the full picture because I'm nothing more than the village bobby."

"You could change that."

"Och, it would mean living in Strathbane and I couldnae bear that."

Hamish relapsed into a moody silence.

The waitress came up to them. "More coffee?"

They both refused. Then she said, "Oh, Mr. Macbeth, Mr. Angus Macdonald was on the phone. He says not to forget the salmon."

"How did he know I was here?"

"Mr. Macdonald always knows."

"Who's Mr. Macdonald?" asked Sarah.

"He's the local seer. He claims to have the second sight."

"And does he?"

"I think he's a verra clever old gossip."

"So what's this about a salmon?"

"He wanted a river salmon, but chust look at the weather. I bought him one in the fishmongers in Braikie and the auld beast sussed out it wass a farm salmon and threatens me with all sorts of bad luck unless I get him the right one."

Sarah looked at him curiously. "How did he know it was a farm salmon?"

"He waved his damn crystal ower it, but I think one o' his gossips phoned him from Braikie."

Sarah looked out at the white wilderness outside. "You certainly won't be able to catch anything in this weather."

"Well, let me get my snowshoes and see if I can make it back to the police station."

When Hamish emerged from the hotel, a couple of tractors with snowploughs attached had cleared the hotel forecourt and even the narrow road outside had already been ploughed and salted. The sky above was steel grey but no snow fell. He trudged down into Lochdubh through the frozen landscape. Everything was still, everything was quiet. No bird sang. Not even a buzzard sailed up to the cold sky. The tops of the twin mountains above Lochdubh were hidden in mist. Fortunately, there was no wind to whip up the snow into another land-blown blizzard.

He checked his sheep and put out their winter fodder. Then he got out a snow shovel and cleared the short drive at the side of the police station so that he could get the Land Rover out.

He then made a thermos of coffee with plenty of milk and sugar, placed it in the Land Rover and drove up to the Tommel Castle Hotel.

He was glad to have Sarah's company.

"I hope the road's clear all the way to Braikie," he said. They were driving along beside the sea as the one-track road twisted and curved. Sarah looked out in amazement at the fury of the green-grey Atlantic. Waves as huge as houses pounded the rocky beach.

"Stop for a moment," she urged.

She looked out of the window in awe at the stormy sea. "It's all so still on land," she marvelled, "and yet the sea is so . . . furious."

"All the way from America," said Hamish.

"Is it always so rough?"

"No, sometimes in the summer it's like glass. But it's a treacherous climate up here."

He let in the clutch and moved off slowly. It was so bitterly cold that despite the salt on the road, he could feel ice under the wheels.

"Where did Gilchrist live?" asked Sarah.

"This end of the town—Culloden Road. Here we are." The Land Rover rolled to a stop after he had made a right turn. "And here we stay." The road was blocked by drifts. "You'd best stay here, Sarah, while I make my way to the house on foot."

"I'll be all right. The snow is so cold and powdery, I won't get wet."

They climbed down. Hamish went ahead, forging a way through the drifts. There was no one on duty outside Gilchrist's house. He correctly guessed that the roads around Strathbane would still be blocked. The further one got from the towns, the better the road-clearing services. It was a Victorian villa of the kind that line so many of the roads in Scotland's towns. After Queen Victoria made the Highlands fashionable, even the lowliest tried to emulate her and so all these villas with grand names like Mount Pleasant, The Pines, The Firs and The Laurels had sprung up. Gilchrist's house was called Culloden House, no doubt allowing anyone who had not seen the villa but only the address on his stationery to envisage a country mansion.

Hamish ploughed his way up the short drive. "Now what are we going to do?" he said, half to himself.

"Let's go round the back," urged Sarah. "There might be something open."

They went round the side of the house, which had been sheltered from the blizzard and so the path was relatively clear.

Hamish rattled the back door. "Of course it's locked and sealed," he grumbled. "And we'll have been seen from the houses around."

"You could say you were investigating a break-in," said Sarah.

He looked down at her and suddenly smiled. "So I could," he remarked cheerfully. He took a short truncheon out of his coat pocket and with one brisk blow smashed the glass panel of the back door, leaned in and unfastened the lock. "So there's the break-in," said Hamish, "and here am I investigating it. And we're shielded from the other houses by the trees and bushes and that high fence. No one will have seen us and och, the sound of glass could have chust been us clearing up the pieces."

They entered the house and found themselves in a modern kitchen. The air was very cold and stale.

"Let's try the living room first."

Hamish walked through to the living room and stood looking around. There was an expensive, white, fitted carpet under his feet. A three-piece suite covered in white leather looked as frozen in all its glacial pristine newness as the snow outside. There was a coffee table with old coins let into the surface. A wall unit contained a stereo, a television set, a few paperbacks and a selection of videos.

A bad oil painting of a Highland scene hung over the fireplace, which had been blocked off and was now fronted by an electric fire with fake logs. There was a desk over at the window. Hamish substituted his thick leather gloves for a pair of thin plastic ones which he had drawn from his pocket and put on. "Don't touch anything without gloves on," he ordered Sarah. He gently drew open the drawers of the desk. There were various letters and bills. The letters were from uninteresting bodies such as the local Rotary Club and from drug suppliers.

He searched on, carefully replacing everything exactly as he found it. "That's odd," he muttered, "no bankbooks, no statements, no credit card records."

"Try the bedroom," whispered Sarah. "Sometimes people keep that sort of stuff beside the bed in a drawer or maybe in a suitcase under the bed."

They went quietly upstairs. One bedroom proved to be a spare one, but the other, containing a large double bed covered with a shiny green silk quilt, had an inhabited look. Hamish opened the wardrobe. Yes, there were the suits and shirts itemised in the report. He turned his attention to the bedside table. He slid open the drawer. There was a Gideon Bible and, underneath it, a few pornographic magazines and a sealed packet of condoms, blackberry flavour.

"They have to be somewhere. Let's see if there's a box room or something like that," said Hamish.

"Don't be long," urged Sarah. "If one of the neighbours heard the breaking glass, we'll soon be in trouble."

Hamish went back out onto the small landing. There were two doors he had not tried.

One proved to be the bathroom and the other, yet another bedroom.

He scratched his fiery hair.

"Wouldn't there be a cellar in a house like this?" asked Sarah behind him.

"Aye, let's go and look. But bank statements and things like that would hardly be put away in a basement."

They went back down to the kitchen and then into the hall. There was a low door under the stairs. Hamish opened it. A narrow wooden staircase led downwards. He made his way down, followed by Sarah.

The detectives for some reason had not thought to write down that in the basement was a well-equipped gym full of expensive weightlifting and exercise equipment. And what was more important, an old-fashioned rolltop desk in one corner.

Hamish made a beeline for it. "Here we are at last," he said. "Accounts, credit card statements, bankbooks." He sat down in front of it. Sarah waited nervously, expecting to hear the wail of a police siren at any moment.

"Now here's a thing," said Hamish after what Sarah felt to be an agonisingly long time. "The man was in debt and bad debt at that. He's got an overdraft of fifty-five thousand pounds at the National Highland, and twenty-five thousand with Tay General. His credit card bills, Visa and Access, are high. I'll just note down which restaurants he went to and maybe we can call there and see who it was he was entertaining. Well, well, well, last o' the big spenders."

"Hamish," pleaded Sarah, "if you've found out what you want, let's get out of here."

"Aye, we'd better move. But I'd better get a glazier to fix thon door."

"But getting a glazier without telling the police first will let them know when they learn of it that you were the one who broke in."

"The man I'm going to ask won't talk. And if he's caught, he can say I broke in because I thought I saw someone moving about inside."

Sarah was glad when they left the house and ploughed their

way back to the Land Rover. Hamish drove off and then stopped at a cottage on the outskirts. "You wait here and I'll tell the glazier what to do. Keep the engine and heater running." After some time he rejoined her. "He'll fix it. He says it was on the radio that all the roads about Strathbane are still blocked so he should have plenty of time."

"Now what?"

"Maggie Bane, I think. That's if the lassie hasnae been arrested."

Maggie Bane answered the door to them. She was dressed in a black sweater and skirt and her face was puffy with crying. Hamish had wondered whether to leave Sarah in the Land Rover, but had decided to take her with him. If Maggie objected to her presence, he could tell Sarah to wait outside.

"I was passing," said Hamish in his light, pleasant Highland accent, "and I wondered how you were getting on. This is not really a police call, more in the way of a friendly call."

"Come in." She led the way to her sterile living room. "Sit down," she said wearily.

Sarah studied Maggie's beautiful face. How on earth could such a good-looking girl become involved with a middle-aged dentist in a bleak Highland town?

"Did you have a hard time at police headquarters?" asked Hamish.

"It was terrible. That brute Blair shouted and yelled at me. I tried to tell him that I had been trying to protect my reputation. This isn't Glasgow or London. This is the Highlands of Scotland."

"If it doesn't distress you too much, could you tell me what the attraction was?" Hamish leaned forward, looking the picture of sympathy.

"He was glamorous."

"A middle-aged dentist?"

"You didn't know him," she said wearily. "I met him in St. Andrews. I was just finishing at university, had just passed my finals. I'm . . . I'm not good at making friends. I went off to a bar to have a drink to celebrate. He was at the bar and we fell into conversation. Then he suddenly said, 'I'm going to Paris tomorrow. Come with me. I'll get your air ticket.'

"And I said, 'Yes,' just like that and it was wonderful. We stayed at the George V and we walked along the quays and looked at the bookshops and he insisted on buying me a hat covered with artificial flowers at the Galerie Lafayette, although I told him no one wore hats anymore." She gave a choked little sob. "I've still got that hat."

There was a silence. Outside, the frozen branch of a tree rapped against the window with monotonous regularity, like an impatient finger.

"And why did your relationship with him break up?"

"We went on holiday to Provence, to Agde and Sète and along that coast. It rained every day. The clouds were so low they seemed to lie on the sea. We were staying at some old château which had been turned into a hotel. It was very expensive but the roof leaked and everything smelled of damp. He became irritable and tetchy and began to pick quarrels. We were meant to be away on holiday for three weeks, but he suddenly cut the holiday short after a week. I cried and cried, but he wouldn't listen to me."

Hamish took a deep breath. "Did it no' dawn on you, lassie," he said gently, "that Mr. Gilchrist might be worried about money?"

Her amazement seemed genuine. "But he earned a very good pay as a dentist. He always had the latest car, dined at the best restaurants."

"Was there another woman?"

"I think there was. I took to following him. Oh, it was silly. He found out right away and said if I didn't give him space, he would have to get rid of me. He went down to Inverness a lot. I'm sure there was someone there."

"If you can think of anything at all," said Hamish, "just phone me. I'll come over right away."

Maggie sniffed miserably. "You're very kind, not like those dreadful policemen in Strathbane."

"Have the press been bothering you?"

"Yes, but this weather will keep them away, and they seem to have lost interest anyway."

"Did Mr. Gilchrist have any particular friends?"

"No, for a time there was just me. Neither of us had any friends up here. We were all we needed."

"And relatives? I mean, as far as I know, no relative has come forward."

"He said he was an only child and that his parents were dead."

"Odd that. You would think there would be a cousin or someone." Wedding photographs, thought Hamish. Jeannie Gilchrist would have wedding photographs. Must see her.

He rose and said goodbye. He was grateful that Maggie had not commented on Sarah's presence.

Once back in the Land Rover, he said, "I'll drop you back at the hotel and go to Inverness. I want to talk to Gilchrist's ex-wife again."

"Take me with you," said Sarah. "I'm not doing anything else."

Hamish looked out at the steel grey sky. "The wind's rising," he said. "It might be a hairy journey."

"Then let's be hairy together."

Hamish smiled at her suddenly. "Inverness it is."

CHAPTER SEVEN

"Well, now that we have *seen each other,"* said the Unicorn, *"if
you'll believe in me, I'll believe in you. Is that a bargain?"*

—Lewis Carroll

"There's coffee in that thermos on the floor beside you," said
Hamish as they drove slowly along. "It's got milk and sugar in
it because I meant to use it to make any policeman on guard
outside Gilchrist's a bit friendlier towards me."

"I don't take sugar, but I may be driven to it if we're trapped
in this snow."

"We'll go over by Dornoch and take the bridge," said
Hamish, peering out into the gloom. "I think the snow's getting
a bit wetter."

By the time they reached the long bridge over the Dornoch
Firth, Hamish's eyes felt tired and gritty with the strain of peering ahead. As they made their way over the bridge, Hamish
could see a yellowish light at the end and wondered what it was.

He soon found out.

On the other side was a different world. They drove straight out of the swirling snow and blackness and into brilliant sunshine. Hamish looked back in his driving mirror in amazement at the black wall of bad weather behind him. "Let's just hope the storm stays where it is," he said, "and doesn't follow us into Inverness."

"I will never get used to this weird climate. What do you hope to find out from Mrs. Gilchrist?" asked Sarah.

"I want to find out all I can about the man. She surely knew him better than anyone else."

"What about Maggie Bane?"

"She was just having the affair with him. Marriage fair brings out the beast in people."

"Yes, it does," she said sadly.

He glanced sharply at the hunched figure in the passenger seat. "What would you know about it?"

"Observation," she said, "just like you."

When they reached Anstruther Road in Inverness, Hamish climbed down from the Land Rover and looked up at the sky. Long ragged trails of black cloud were streaming out from the west, the fingers of the storm clawing eastward.

Jeannie Gilchrist was not at home. "Of course, she'll be back at work," said Hamish. "Let's go into Inverness and get something to eat and then we'll try the council offices."

They found a self-service cafe. Sarah had a salad and Hamish, a Scotch pie and chips.

"You don't worry about your cholesterol level, I see," remarked Sarah.

"It's comfort food," said Hamish. "Salad makes me tetchy."

"I cannot imagine you getting tetchy," said Sarah. "You seem much too laid-back."

He smiled at her. "I have the vicious temper."

"I don't believe that. Look at all the people inside and out.

Where do they all come from? I was amazed to find Inverness such a busy place."

"Aye, it's grown out o' recognition. There's something suddenly bothering me."

"And what's that?"

"Thon still o' the Smiley brothers. I keep thinking of that long shed. I mean a few bottles here and there for the locals is all right. What if they were into big production?"

"You keep saying it's hard to keep anything quiet in the Highlands. Someone would have told you. I mean, you said that Kylie girl in the chemists knew about them."

"I suppose that's true. Well, murder comes before illegal hooch."

After their meal, they went to the council offices and found Jeannie Gilchrist. She led them into a side room. Hamish introduced Sarah, saying she was a friend he had met in Inverness and that she could wait outside if Jeannie objected to her presence. Jeannie shrugged. "I've no secrets. I will have to cope with Frederick's funeral after the procurator fiscal releases the body."

"That's why I'm here. He had no wedding photographs or photographs of any kind in his house. There must have been some relatives at the wedding."

"Oh, that's easily explained. He hated photographs of himself. I think he carried a glamorised picture of himself in his head and didn't like to look at the reality. He was very vain. There were no relatives at the wedding. He was actually adopted from an orphanage. The couple who adopted him are long dead. He had a few colleagues at the wedding."

"You said something to me about thinking he might have been married before. Surely that would have come out in his papers when you were making the wedding arrangements."

"He handled all that. No, I suppose he was never married before if there's no evidence of it. It was just a feeling, an intuition that one time he had been heavily involved with someone and that no one else was ever going to match up."

Hamish sighed. "Every time I think I've found something mysterious and significant, it's all explained neatly away. I happen to know he was heavily in debt."

"Finally caught up with him, did it?"

"What?"

"He liked to show off, big car, best restaurants, that kind of man."

"Did you know he was having an affair with his receptionist, Maggie Bane?"

"I did not. But then I never saw or heard from him."

"Mrs. Gilchrist, someone hated him enough to kill him in a savage way. Can you guess what he might have got into?"

She shook her head. "He was a braggart and a show-off but he was never involved in anything criminal."

"Why do you assume that the murderer or murderers were criminals?"

"The drilling the teeth. That could have been a form of revenge."

"Yes," said Hamish slowly. "So it could."

He could not think of anything else to ask her and so they took their leave. Once outside, he said, "That still is bothering me. I'll drop you back at the hotel. No, I can't take you with me. The Smiley brothers can be nasty." He cocked his head to one side. "The Inverness seagulls have stopped screaming overhead and the sky is black. I wonder if we can make it back."

They crossed the suspension bridge over the Black Isle and took the A9 north. Snowflakes began to whirl about them and the road in front was becoming whiter by the minute.

"This is hopeless," said Hamish. "I think I'll take the road over to Dingwall and find us a place to stay."

"All right," said Sarah.

Traffic had slowed to a crawl. They seemed to inch their way towards the town of Dingwall through the thickening, driving sheets of snow. Hamish finally drove up to the Station Hotel and parked.

At reception, he asked for two rooms. "Two," said the receptionist, peering over the desk at Sarah's wrists.

She grinned. "No handcuffs. I am a friend of Mr. Macbeth, not a prisoner."

After they had been shown to adjoining rooms, Sarah insisted on battling out in the storm to a nearby chemists to buy makeup and a toothbrush and toothpaste. They also bought paperbacks and then retreated to the hotel lounge. But while Sarah read, Hamish looked idly out at the driving snow and turned all that he knew about the case over in his mind. Who was the most likely suspect? Maggie Bane. But how could Maggie Bane lift a man as heavy as the dentist and put him in the chair?

Then there was the deranged Mrs. Harrison. Could she have suffered from an extreme fit of madness that gave her unnatural strength? Or had the dentist been having an affair with Kylie— Kylie who knew so many young men in the bar?

There was a sudden vicious pattering against the glass of the lounge windows. "It's turning to rain," commented one of the guests.

Sarah looked up from her book. "If it thaws quickly, we might not have to stay here for the night."

"Oh, I should think whateffer happens, the roads will be much too bad to move in the night," said Hamish.

She returned to her book. Hamish studied her speculatively. Her shiny brown hair shielded her face. Here they were in a romantic situation, stranded in this hotel by the station. Was there any hope for Hamish Macbeth?

Perhaps it would be better to go on thinking about the murder and stop wondering whether he could get her into bed or not.

They had an early dinner. Rain was now falling heavily. They went out for a walk after dinner. The air was full of rushing water.

"Look, the road is clear," said Sarah.

"Aye, but we'd best leave things to the morning," said Hamish. "It could still be snowing farther north."

When they returned to the hotel, Sarah said she was going to have a bath and go to bed and read. Hamish rather bleakly said good night to her. So much for a romantic evening!

In his room, he stripped off, washed his underwear and shirt and hung them up to dry. Then he had a bath and climbed into bed and settled down to read, trying to forget about Sarah in the next room. He had succeeded so well that when there was a knock on his door, he called out, "Come in!" thinking it to be one of the hotel staff. "It's not locked."

The door opened and Sarah came in. She was wrapped in a blanket.

"I couldn't sleep," she said. She stood there, looking at him.

He sat up and pulled back the bedclothes. "Come and join me."

She dropped the blanket. She was naked underneath it. She got into bed beside Hamish. He opened his mouth to say something but she put her hand across it. "No questions," she whispered. "Let's make love."

When Hamish awoke in the morning, sun was streaming in through the windows and Sarah had gone. What was it about women, he thought crossly, that they were able to wake early after a night of lovemaking and disappear?

He had another bath and dressed and then knocked on her

bedroom door. There was no reply. He went down to the dining room. Sarah was halfway through breakfast.

"You looked so peaceful, I didn't like to wake you," she said cheerfully.

"You look remarkably well," said Hamish, who felt exhausted. He looked at her curiously. "Do you usually carry a packet of condoms about with you?"

"I bought them in the chemists while you were looking for a toothbrush."

"That was verra thoughtful of you. How do you feel?"

"Marvellous."

He looked into her eyes but could see nothing more there than the glow of good health. He had an uneasy feeling that he had been used as some sort of gymnastic exercise.

He wanted to say something loverlike but felt inhibited by her cheerful, matter-of-fact attitude.

"It looks as if we'll get back all right," he said. "I'd best go and phone Strathbane in case they're looking for me. I'd best not say I'm in Inverness or they'll ask me what I was doing there."

"You can tell them you went back to see Mrs. Gilchrist."

"I'm a humble copper. I wasn't even supposed to see her in the first place."

He went through to the reception where there was a public phone and got through to Jimmy Anderson.

"Nothing's been happening," said Jimmy. "Nobody could move here because of the snow."

Relieved to find out that Blair had not been looking for him or had even been back to Braikie, Hamish returned to the dining room.

He had coffee and toast and then suggested that they should make a move.

They were both silent for most of the journey back. Hamish

longed to ask Sarah if their night together had meant anything to her, but was terrified of rejection, terrified of being told brightly that it was only a one-night stand.

He dropped her at the Tommel Castle Hotel and then drove to the police station. The air smelled dusty and stale. He went around opening windows.

He checked on his hens and sheep, changed his clothes and climbed back into the police Land Rover. Time to visit the Smiley brothers.

The road was atrocious, thick with slush and grit. But a mild wind blew from the west and the sky was a washed-out blue with trailing wisps of white cloud. There was an air of false spring in the air, bringing with it the thoughts that spring usually brings. But he clamped down on any thoughts about Sarah Hudson as soon as they arose.

As he bumped up the rutted track that led to the Smileys' croft house, he could sense those troll eyes watching him.

Stourie came round the side of the house and stood watching as Hamish descended from the Land Rover and walked towards him. Stourie was joined by Pete.

"What brings ye?" demanded Stourie.

"I want a look at your lambing shed."

"Do you haff the search warrant?"

"Don't be silly," snapped Hamish. "You want me to go and get a search warrant then I will. But I'll need to tell Strathbane exactly why I want it and you'll be arrested, for it seems well known you run a still."

"Chust our wee joke," said Stourie with a hideous smile. He had his dreadful dentures in that morning. "Come along."

He led the way to the new extension. He took a large key from his pocket and unlocked the door.

Hamish stepped into the gloom of the shed. It just looked

like an ordinary lambing shed. But why the shuttered windows? He searched about but could see nothing suspicious.

"There's one more thing," he said, "I'll need to be examining that still of yours."

"Och, Hamish, we're no' daft," jeered Stourie. "The minute we knew you wass on to us, we smashed the whole thing up."

"I find that hard to believe."

"Well, chust believe it," snapped Peter. "We've enough to dae on the croft anyways."

Hamish insisted on searching their house, but there was no sign of a still anywhere.

He left with a feeling that he had been conned. But then, was it likely the Smiley brothers, who had no contact with Gilchrist, would have poisoned him? There was no motive.

Feeling low, Hamish drove back to Lochdubh. He took the salmon that the seer had not wanted out of the fridge and poached it in a fish kettle. Then he divided it up into steaks and put them in the freezer.

The phone in the office rang and he went to answer it. "This is Kylie Fraser," said the voice. "I want you to come to my flat this evening. I've got something to tell you about Gilchrist."

"Tell me now."

"No, this evening at eleven. It's number fifteen, Wick Road." She rang off. Hamish looked thoughtfully at his own receiver before replacing it.

What was going on? Kylie's voice had sounded excited, a tinge malicious, not frightened or anxious, and he was sure he could hear someone giggling in the background.

There was a knock at the kitchen door. He opened it and his heart leapt with gladness when he saw Sarah standing there, smiling up at him.

"I've brought you a present," she said, holding out a plastic-wrapped package.

"Come in." She followed him into the kitchen. "Don't bother unwrapping it," she said. "It's a river salmon. Wild salmon. For the seer. Save you poaching."

"Where did you get it?"

"Mr. Johnson said he had salmon in the hotel freezer, caught in the river. I had an ulterior motive anyway. I want to visit this seer."

"We may as well go now," said Hamish. "I went to the Smiley brothers and they said they had smashed the still. He may have heard something."

He hesitated a moment. He wanted to take her in his arms but she was emanating that sort of hard, brisk cheerfulness which made him afraid to try.

The seer was at home—he hardly ever went out. It was not as if he had to shop for anything, thought Hamish. The old fraud emotionally blackmailed so many of his "clients" into supplying him with goods.

Sarah was obviously thrilled with Angus and his old cottage. Angus accepted the salmon but Hamish noticed that he did not go to fetch his crystal, merely said, "Glad to have it at last," and put it away in the kitchen.

He served them tea and then sat down and looked with bright eyes from Hamish to Sarah. "I suppose," he said, "I cannot blame you for grabbing a wee bit o' happiness."

"I neffer know what you're on about, Angus," said Hamish repressively. "Now, I went to the Smileys' and they told me they had smashed that still. I thought that new building they call a lambing shed might have been a place where they were manufacturing the stuff, but it looks like nothing more than a regular lambing shed."

"Aye, well, that must be the case," said Angus. "It iss the

cauld day, Miss Hudson. Would you be liking a wee drap o'
something in your tea?"

"I think I would, thank you," said Sarah, saving up every
moment of this odd experience to tell her friends back in London. Would they believe there were still places in the British
Isles where someone heated the kettle hung on a chain over a
peat fire?

Angus produced a bottle of Johnnie Walker and poured a
slug of the contents into Sarah's cup.

"What do you know about a wee lassie called Kylie Fraser
who works for the chemist in Braikie?" asked Hamish.

"Flirty wee thing, by all accounts," said Angus.

"She says she has something to tell me and has asked me to
go to her flat at eleven o'clock this evening."

"I know you haff been asking the questions about her and
the dentist and I know she didn't like that," said Angus.

Hamish's hazel eyes narrowed. "So you think the idea is I go
there and she's got some of her thug boyfriends waiting for
me?"

"I wouldnae think she would do that," said Angus. "It's not
the city. No one up here would beat up a copper."

"So what's behind it?"

Angus half closed his eyes. "I cannae see clearly. The fact iss
that it iss so cold here that I cannae think straight. Have you
see those fine warm mohair travelling rugs in the gift shop at
Tommel Castle, Miss Hudson? I've always fancied one of
those."

Hamish stood up abruptly. "Ignore that, Sarah. Your
mooching is getting worse, Angus. A man can't have a few moments' conversation with you, but you're asking for something."

"Did I ask for anything?" demanded the seer huffily. "All I
said was—"

"Come along, Sarah," said Hamish.

Sarah followed Hamish reluctantly from the cottage. "I thought he was a fascinating old man, Hamish. I would have liked to stay longer." He opened the door of the Land Rover for her and then went round and climbed into the driver's seat.

"I have to live with these people, Sarah, you don't. I'll take you back to the hotel and then I'll think what to do about this evening."

As he drove, he hoped she would ask if they were having dinner together, but she was very silent. In the hotel forecourt, she suddenly put her hand to her head. "I would ask you in for a coffee, Hamish, but I've got this awful stabbing headache. I think I'll go and lie down."

"Right you are," said Hamish grimly, thinking, couldn't she find a less hackneyed excuse than a headache. He was just driving off when he suddenly slammed on the brakes, reversed into the car park, jumped down from the Land Rover and rushed into the hotel.

Sarah was just going up the stairs. "Sarah!" he called. She turned round.

"Go into the bar and have a whisky—quickly. It's the only cure for that headache. Can't wait."

Hamish rushed off again. He drove straight back to the seer's.

"I know why you're so anxious to let me believe that lambing shed was straightforward," he said. "The Smiley brothers have been supplying you with their hooch."

"And what gives you that idea?"

"Sarah's headache. She got it from thon whisky you poured in her cup."

"That wass Johnnie Walker."

"It was a Johnnie Walker label. Where's the bottle?"

"In the kitchen."

Hamish went through to the kitchen, which was a lean-to

attached to the back of the cottage. A rinsed-out, clean and empty Johnnie Walker bottle stood on the draining board.

"You threw away the proof," he said, coming back into the living room. "If you know anything, Angus . . ."

"I only know what the spirits tell me," said the seer, his eyes bright with malice.

Hamish made a sound of disgust and strode out. As he drove back to the police station, he conjured up a mental picture of that lambing shed. But there had been nothing sinister about it, nothing at all. He would put it to the back of his mind and concentrate on what to do that evening about Kylie Fraser.

Now, if he were a regular citizen, thinking of how to deal with a young woman who seemed to be in some kind of trouble, he would not go alone. He would take his wife. A slow smile curved his lips. He walked along to the manse and found Mrs. Wellington, the minister's tweedy wife, at home.

"I have a wee problem," said Hamish, "and wanted to ask your advice."

"You've been messing around with that pretty tourist."

"I have not!" Hamish coloured up, a sudden vision of tumbled naked bodies in a hotel bed crashing into his mind. "It iss the other matter."

"What matter?"

"There is a girl over in Braikie, Kylie Fraser."

"That saucy piece. Oh, Hamish, and to think you could have had Priscilla."

"*I am not involved with Kylie Fraser!*" shouted Hamish, exasperated. "And if you won't chust listen to me like a sensible woman, I'm out of here."

"Sorry, Hamish, but you do have a bit of a reputation. Go on."

"It's like this. I thought that Kylie Fraser might have been having a fling with Gilchrist, the murdered dentist. She phoned me this morning, asking me to call on her in her flat at eleven o'clock this evening because she said she had something to tell me. Now," Hamish went on, pinning a pious expression on his face, "normally I would ask Strathbane for a policewoman to accompany me, but, och, it hass been my experience that the policewomen in Strathbane would be apt to frighten a girl like Kylie, whereas a woman of good sense like yourself, and the minister's wife, too, might be the very person to go with me."

"I take a strong line with girls like Kylie."

"Chust what I thought," murmured Hamish. "Would you be free this evening?"

"I have a mothers' meeting this evening at the church hall, but it would be finished by ten."

"So you'll come with me?"

"Yes, I would consider it my Christian duty."

"Good," said Hamish. "I'll pick you up at ten-thirty."

"I will follow you in my car," said Mrs. Wellington severely. "Members of the public should not be in a police vehicle. Which brings me to something I have heard . . ."

"Got to go," said Hamish, heading for the door. "I'll be here at ten-thirty."

He strolled back to the police station. The air was becoming colder and the wind was shifting round from the west to the north. He hoped there would not be another storm.

The phone in the police office was ringing and he went to answer it. It was Sarah.

"That cure of yours worked like a charm," she said, "and then I remembered you telling me about the effect of the Smiley brothers' whisky and that brought a little thing to mind. I'm sure it's not important but it happened when I was at The Scotsman Hotel."

"What's that?"

"Mrs. Macbean went up to the bar and asked for a whisky and said, 'Give me the decent stuff.' It may be nothing at all."

"But The Scotsman could be stocking hooch and putting it into regular bottles on the gantry. If the Smiley brothers were supplying the hotels, that would mean a major operation. I turned a blind eye to it because I thought they were running the usual Highland still, a few bottles for themselves and their friends," said Hamish.

"Do you want me to go out there and ask for a whisky and see if I get a headache?"

"Too risky. They've seen you before. I'll send someone else."

There was a little silence.

Then Hamish said tentatively, "I don't need to leave until ten-thirty this evening. Any chance of us having dinner together?"

"Not tonight. I'm expecting a call from London."

"Oh, well in that case . . ."

"Maybe tomorrow, Hamish. There's always tomorrow."

"Bye." He rang off and sat looking sadly out at the loch. In this modern age, he could not ask things like, "Did our night together mean nothing to you?"

Well, of course he could, but the answer might be a simple no and he felt he would not be able to bear that.

He went down to the Lochdubh bar and found Archie Macleod. "I want you to do a wee favour for me, Archie."

"I hivnae had much sleep, Hamish. I was going to have a snooze this afternoon."

"It won't take long. I'll pay you. I'll pay you to drink."

"That's different."

"Okay. Here's what I want you to do . . ."

Archie strolled into the bar of The Scotsman Hotel an hour later. The barman, Johnny King, looked with contempt at the little fisherman in his tight, shiny suit. "What's your pleasure, *sir?*" he asked with a sneer in his voice.

"I'll hae a shot o' Bells," said Archie, pointing to a bottle on the gantry. The barman held the bottle under the optic and then put the glass down on the bar. Archie paid with the money Hamish had given him, and tossed the measure back in one gulp. "Anything else?" asked Johnny.

"No, I'll be on my way." Archie headed for the door. Nothing. He felt fine. Whistling cheerfully, he went out into the car park. Then he stopped and clutched his head as pain stabbed through it. He opened his car door and fished a half bottle of Bells that Hamish had given him out of the glove compartment and took a swig of it. The pain in his head miraculously disappeared. Archie drove off to Lochdubh and straight to the police station.

"Grand," said Hamish. "Don't be telling a soul about this, Archie. I'll bet those brothers haven't destroyed the still at all."

"Are ye sure it isnae a wee bottle here and a wee bottle there, Hamish? If it were a big operation, someone would have talked afore this."

"If it were a big operation," said Hamish slowly, "they'd be verra quiet about it, and those in the know wouldnae dare talk. I think those Smiley boys are nasty customers."

"So are ye going to raid them?"

"I think I'd better get some more proof. Anyway, if I got that whole lot over from Strathbane, the Smileys would hear of their coming afore they even left the town."

"I'll ask about, Hamish. Someone might let something slip."

"All right, Archie, thanks. But be careful."

Hamish then phoned Jimmy Anderson. "Are you any farther forward wi' the investigations?" he asked.

"Full stop, Hamish. Someone's been at Blair's computer again. But when he went to complain to the super about it, the super got a bit worried about Blair's mental state because the man was reeking o' whisky."

"Probably nobody's been near his records," said Hamish. "I thought Blair didn't know one end of a computer from another and was always getting one of the girls to type up his notes for him."

"Aye, that's what the super says so nothing's being done about it this time."

"What about the burglary at The Scotsman?"

"Dead full stop there as well, although it looks as if Macbean'll probably get the insurance money anyway."

"How come?"

"The company that owns the hotel have got hotshot lawyers who are pointing out that a robbery is a robbery and even if the safe hadn't had a wooden back, the burglar or burglars obviously knew what they were doing and that the money was there and so would have taken it anyway. Also the company has all their hotels insured with the same insurance company and they don't want to lose their custom. Well, it's not as if Macbean keeps the insurance money himself. It'll go to a prize for the annual bingo night. So it's not as if he stole the stuff himself and then meant to keep the insurance money."

"Grant me patience," moaned Hamish. "He could have stolen the money himself, kept it, reported the robbery, the company gets the money back from the insurance people and Macbean keeps the money he stole."

"Aye, I suppose so. I wasnae thinking straight."

"Have you gone thoroughly into Macbean's background?"

"Wi' a fine-tooth comb."

"What about Mrs. Macbean, and the barman, Johnny King?"

"All there is tae know about Johnny King, I've already told ye."

"And Mrs. Macbean?"

"Like I told you, born in Leith, bright at school, wouldn't think it to look at her, would you? Used to be a looker, too. Policeman down there was questioning friends and relatives. Saw a photograph of her, Miss Leith 1970. He said she was a stunner."

"What did she work at before she met Macbean?"

"Worked as a secretary."

"Where?"

"Oh, for heaven's sake, man. What does it matter? You'll be saying next, a wee woman like that could murder a man like Gilchrist."

"I know it seems daft. But Mrs. Macbean went to Gilchrist and got all her teeth removed."

"So do a lot of people. You're barking up the wrong tree, Hamish. That murder was committed by brutal men and strong men at that."

"Someone did it," said Hamish. "And that someone's wandering about loose and may kill again. What about Gilchrist's finances?" asked Hamish, as if he did not know the answer. "Was he well-to-do?"

"No, he was in deep debt. So what are you suggesting? That he went over to The Scotsman and pinched the money?"

"I know it seems daft. But I can't help feeling there's a connection somewhere."

"Don't worry, Hamish. We'll get there. Someone's bound to talk, sooner or later."

"The thing that worries me," said Hamish, "is that by that time whoever did the murder could be long gone."

He rang off.

The evening before he was to meet Mrs. Wellington stretched out before him. He defrosted a salmon steak and grilled it for his dinner. Why did Sarah not want to see him?

He could swear she had enjoyed her night with him. Perhaps she was just one of those women who wanted to sleep with a policeman out of curiosity. He should phone Priscilla and tell her about why they had needed her computer, but was reluctant to do so. For one brief glorious night, Sarah had seemed like his passport away from memories of Priscilla and feeling bound to Priscilla.

The wind moaned along the loch. He went back to the office and looked down at the silent phone. He suddenly wanted to call Sarah and ask her what she was playing at.

Then he gave a little shrug. Perhaps tomorrow.

Perhaps he would ask her tomorrow.

Mr. Johnson looked up as Sarah came into the hotel office. "What can I do for you, Miss Hudson?"

"I suppose the gift shop is closed."

"Yes, it's after hours. Was there anything you wanted in particular?"

"I wanted to buy one of those mohair travelling rugs."

Mr. Johnson reached behind him and took a key down from a board on the wall. "I'm not very busy. I'll take you over to the shop."

"Oh, thank you," said Sarah. "And then I would like to borrow one of the hotel cars. I think I have done enough walking for one holiday."

"Certainly," said Mr. Johnson. "First, let's get that rug."

Half an hour later, Angus Macdonald, the seer, heard the sound of a car engine and lumbered over to his cottage window.

Sarah Hudson was climbing out of a car, a mohair travelling rug over one arm.

The seer gave a satisfied little smile and went to open the door.

CHAPTER EIGHT

"Yes," I answered you last night;
"No," this morning, sir, I say.
Colours seen by candle-light
Will not look the same by day.

—Robert Browning

Hamish drove out towards Braikie with Mrs. Wellington follow-ing in her Fiat. He hoped he was doing the right thing. If Kylie re-ally had something important to tell him, she might not want to say anything in front of Mrs. Wellington. But he felt in his bones that Kylie had taken exception to his questions about her. Kylie was obviously used to thinking of herself as the glamour queen of Braikie, a sexy big fish in a very little pool. She did not know that her power came from her youth and when youth had gone, it would leave Kylie—like so many other Kylies he had known—a bitter and bad-tempered woman.

He stopped at the end of the street where Kylie lived and Mrs. Wellington drew in behind him.

He got out of the police Land Rover and walked back to the minister's wife.

"Why are we stopping here?" she asked.

"I don't want her to get a look at you. Might scare her. Let me walk along first and follow me a few yards behind. Don't let yourself be seen from the house. I'll knock at the door. Then when I signal to you, you walk up quickly and go in first."

"What is this? Are you expecting an armed ambush? It would be just like you to hide behind a woman. I've always said—"

"Oh, shut up," said Hamish crossly. "I am trying to help this wee lassie and you are the very person to do it. Like I said, I don't want to frighten her off."

"Very well," said Mrs. Wellington, straightening another of her formidable felt hats. "But never again tell me to shut up, Hamish Macbeth. I don't know what has happened to manners these days."

Hamish sighed. "Now, now, I'm sorry. Come along."

He walked in front of her past a silent row of villas, most of them divided up into flats.

He turned in at Kylie's gate and flashed his torch at the name plates. Kylie Fraser was on the ground floor. He rang the bell. A buzzer went and he entered a hall. The door to Kylie's flat was on the left. He knocked at it.

"Who is it?" came Kylie's voice.

"Hamish Macbeth."

"Just walk in. The door isn't locked."

Hamish darted to the street door and signalled frantically. The bulk of Mrs. Wellington appeared from around the shelter of a hedge. She hurried up the garden path and joined Hamish in the hall.

Hamish indicated Kylie's door. "Go straight on in," he whispered.

Mrs. Wellington squared her shoulders and opened the door and marched in.

Kylie and the minister's wife stared at each other in horror.

Kylie was wearing nothing but a black lace teddy and scarlet high-heeled shoes.

Her mouth fell open.

"Who are you?" she screeched. "Where's Hamish?"

"So this is what you're up to," said Mrs. Wellington belligerently, putting her large handbag down on a table. "Trying to seduce a policeman."

"I never . . ."

Hamish appeared behind Mrs. Wellington and grinned at the sight of Kylie.

"So who's hiding in here ready to rush out and cry 'Rape!'?" he demanded.

"I don't know what you're talking about," said Kylie, but her eyes flickered to a door at the other side of the room.

Hamish strode across the room and jerked that door open. Kylie's friend, Tootsie, and two youths nearly fell into the room.

"Do you mean," boomed Mrs. Wellington, "that this was meant to be some sort of entrapment?"

"I think Kylie was going to rip open the little she has on and scream and her witnesses would then swear I had attacked her," said Hamish.

"If you knew this," said Mrs. Wellington wrathfully, "then you should have brought in some backup."

All these police series on television, thought Hamish, had everyone talking a sort of bastard police lingo.

"But as I am here," said Mrs. Wellington, "I want you young people to sit down and listen to me. I am the minister's wife and it is my Christian duty to bring the error of your ways to your attention. Sit down!"

They meekly sat down while she proceeded to lecture them

on the lack of morals in the younger generation until Hamish interrupted her. "I think they get the message," he said. "Now, Kylie, what was there between you and Gilchrist?"

"Nothing," she said sulkily.

"And yet the very fact that I have been asking questions about you and Gilchrist is enough for you to try to get me charged with rape."

"It was just a joke, that's all," said Kylie.

"It's a joke I don't like, so I am about to drive you to police headquarters where you will be charged with wasting police time, attempting to coerce an officer of the law and God knows what else."

Kylie began to cry, her vamp makeup running down her cheeks.

"Och, I'll tell you," said Tootsie, "if you promise not to charge her."

"I can't promise anything," said Hamish. "But if you are open and honest with me, I'll think about it."

Mrs. Wellington snapped open her capacious handbag and produced a packet of tissues which she handed to Kylie.

"Go on, Kylie," urged Tootsie. "Tell him, or I will."

Kylie blew her nose and then scrubbed at her face. Clean of makeup, her face looked much younger and almost vulnerable.

"Mr. Gilchrist took me out to Inverness a few times, posh restaurants. It was a bit o' a laugh. Then the last time—"

"When was that?" asked Hamish sharply.

"A month ago. He stopped the car on the road back from Inverness and he was all over me. He said I had cost him enough and it was time to pay back. I told him to get stuffed and he slapped me across the face—hard. I said I would tell everyone in Braikie and he seemed to get frightened. He says to me, he says, that if I kept my mouth shut, he would buy me a car."

And where did he plan to get the money for that, wondered Hamish.

"So I kept quiet, but when I called on him and I says, 'Well, where's the car?,' he told me, 'What car,' so I said I would tell everyone and he said I was the town tart and no one would believe me."

"So why didn't you just tell me this?" demanded Hamish. "Why go in for this stupid trick?"

Kylie and her friends stared at him in mulish silence.

"You should charge them," said Mrs. Wellington.

"I don't think there's any need for that, Mrs. Wellington," said Hamish. "But these young people are in need of spiritual guidance, so I'll just be waiting outside while you give them some."

Mrs. Wellington snapped open her huge handbag again and drew out a Bible. As Hamish left, he could hear her voice booming away.

He stood outside the gate and looked up at the burning, bright Sutherland stars.

Gilchrist had been a philanderer. Therefore it followed, it could have been a crime of passion, perhaps committed by some furious husband or lover. Could Kylie have got some of the local youth to do it for her? Hardly. They would have beat him up and spray-painted the walls of his surgery, that was more their style.

He thought again about the Smiley brothers. Whether their still had been used to make nicotine poison was something to be considered. After he escorted Mrs. Wellington home, he would drive back to the Smileys' croft and see if there was any sign of activity.

After some time, Mrs. Wellington emerged. "I think I have talked some sense into their immoral heads. But how did you guess, Hamish, what she had planned for you?"

"Just a feeling," said Hamish.

After he had followed her to the manse and seen her safely indoors, he went back to the police station and changed into a black sweater and black trousers and then set out on the Braikie road again.

He parked the Land Rover some way away from the Smileys' property and continued on foot.

The night was very quiet. He went along the side of the new extension and stopped at the door. He flicked his pencil torch at the padlock. It was open. He quietly opened the door and let himself into the darkness of the shed. He flashed the torch around. It looked just as it had been before, but this time he began to search the place inch by inch, pausing every so often to cock his head and listen in case he heard some movement from outside. He had almost given up when he impatiently kicked aside the straw in a pen in the corner. A large new-looking trapdoor was revealed underneath.

With a smile of triumph, he lifted the heavy hasp and swung the trapdoor open. A flight of wooden steps led downwards. He went quietly down the stairs, stood at the bottom and flashed the light around.

A huge still occupied one corner, pipes and vats and barrels and a whole bottling plant.

Got you, thought Hamish.

His torch flicked over the size of the still. It seemed too huge an apparatus to make a little nicotine poison.

Satisfied, he backed towards the trapdoor. This could not wait until the morning. He would return to the police station and get a squad over from Strathbane.

And then just as he had nearly reached the stairs, there was an almighty crash as the trapdoor was slammed down.

He darted up the stairs. "Stourie! Pete!" he yelled. "Open this door at once!"

But the only answer was the sound of retreating footsteps.

He went up the stairs and pushed at the trapdoor above his head but he could not even budge it an inch. He shouted and yelled and banged. There was nothing now but silence.

Hamish was suddenly frightened. Did the Smileys plan to leave him down here to rot? There was the police Land Rover parked down the road, but what if they knew how to hot-wire it to get it started. And no one knew where he was.

Sarah Hudson banged on the door of the police station and then went round and knocked on Hamish's bedroom window. She had been unable to sleep. She had felt that she had treated Hamish Macbeth very badly and had decided that as the night was cold but fine that she would go down and wake him up and take matters from there. But there was no reply and the police station had that empty atmosphere any building has when the resident is away from home.

Feeling dejected, she turned and began to walk along the waterfront, keeping to the shadow of the cottages, for she suddenly wondered what any local might think of her, if she was seen.

She heard the sound of a vehicle approaching and pressed back into the Currie sisters' privet hedge.

The police Land Rover passed her followed by a truck. So Hamish wasn't alone.

She waited in the darkness of the hedge. Then the truck, this time with two men in it, came past her.

She watched it disappear and then headed back to the police station. The Land Rover stood at the side of the building. But there were no lights on in the police station. Surely Hamish wasn't creeping off to bed in the dark.

She went to the kitchen door and knocked. Silence.

She stood there, her hand to her mouth. What was going

on? Was Hamish off on some secret assignment? Had two fellow officers driven the Land Rover back for him?

She tried the handle of the kitchen door. Locked.

But someone as easygoing as Hamish was the type of man who probably usually forgot his keys. Had he left one around under a flower pot or in the gutter the way country people often still did?

She stood on tiptoe and ran her hand along the guttering on the low roof but found nothing. She dropped to her knees and peered around in the darkness and then lifted away the doormat and felt the ground underneath with her fingers.

Those fingers closed on a key. "Now let's see if I can find out what's going on," she muttered.

She unlocked the door, went in and shouted, "Hamish!" at the top of her voice. No answer. She searched through the small station, ending up in the office and looking through the papers and notes on the desk for some clue.

And then all at once she remembered Hamish saying he wanted to find out about the Smiley brothers and saying they could be dangerous.

She then stared at the phone. "I hope I'm doing the right thing," she said aloud, "or Hamish will never forgive me." She looked up the phone number of police headquarters at Strathbane and began to dial.

She was put through to a tired Jimmy Anderson, who was on night duty. He listened carefully to her story about the suspected still, the Smiley brothers, and then how two men had driven the Land Rover, parked it outside the police station and left.

"I'll see to it," said Jimmy. "Why didn't the silly fool tell us about this?"

"He said that with the noise you lot made arriving from

Strathbane, the Smiley brothers would get to hear of it before you even left."

"Aye, he had a point there," said Jimmy. "But we'll be careful."

"Be quick," urged Sarah. "He may be in danger."

Hamish had fallen into an uneasy sleep when he suddenly awoke. Someone was opening the trapdoor. He made a dash for the stairs. A shotgun was being pointed straight at him through the trapdoor.

"Back off, Hamish," came Stourie's voice, "or I'll blast your head off." He pressed a switch by the stairs and the cellar was flooded with harsh light.

Stourie eased his way down the stairs followed by Pete. "Tie him up and gag him," Stourie instructed his brother.

"People know I'm here," said Hamish desperately.

"Aye, well, if they knew you were here, where are they?" sneered Smiley. "We all know you fancy yoursel' as the Lone Ranger. Tie him up, Pete."

Hamish was trussed up, and a broad piece of sticking plaster was pasted over his mouth.

"That's him dealt with," said Pete. "What do we do now?"

"Wait till the fuss dies down and make sure no one comes here looking for him and then we'll drop the cratur in the nearest peat bog."

"Aye, that'll do fine," said Pete. He stretched and yawned. "I'm dead tired. Let's get some sleep." He gave the trussed Hamish a vicious kick in the ribs.

Then both brothers went up the stairs, switching off the light and leaving Hamish Macbeth lying on the floor, helpless in the darkness.

✶   ✶   ✶

It was dawn before police and detectives began to spread out over the moors outside the Smileys' croft.

Blair roused from his bed was in a foul mood. "Close in," he said. "That girlfriend o' Macbeth's said it was that shed he was interested in."

Inside the croft house, a dog began to bark furiously. "That's it!" shouted Blair. "Go for it! Fast!"

Men smashed in the door of the shed, just as the Smileys erupted from their house. "What the hell's going on here?" shouted Stourie.

Blair went up to him. "We believe you are holding a police-man." And let's hope these weird-looking buggers have killed him, thought Blair suddenly. A life without Hamish Macbeth. Bloody marvellous.

"Whit policeman?" asked Stourie.

"Call off your dogs," shouted Blair as two dogs snapped at his ankles.

"Down boys," growled Stourie. "You're going to have to pay for the damage to that lock."

Blair grunted by way of reply and walked into the shed and looked around. "Nothing here," said Jimmy.

"Ach, I should have known it," said Blair, his voice heavy with disgust. "Hamish and his hysterical women. And do you know the price o' this operation? We'll search the house any-way. Come on men. Nothing here."

Downstairs, Hamish heard him. In desperation he twisted and wriggled across the floor and kicked out savagely with his bound feet at a row of bottles.

"What was that?" said Jimmy Anderson at the doorway of the shed.

"I heard nothing," said Stourie.

Silence again.

"Come on!" snapped Blair.

Crash!

"Jesus, it's coming from under the floor. There's a base-ment."

"There is not." A film of sweat covered Stourie's face despite the cold of the dawn.

"Search all over the floor," howled Blair. He had been so anxious to prove that Hamish Macbeth's girlfriend had insti-gated a useless and expensive search that he had called off the search too soon.

"Over here," called a policeman, scraping aside the straw over the trapdoor.

Blair lumbered over. "Unlock it," he said over his shoulder to Stourie.

"I dinnae hae a key," howled Stourie.

Blair nodded to a policeman who came forward with a sledgehammer and brought it down on the lock and smashed it.

The trapdoor was thrown back. Blair went down. Behind him Jimmy Anderson had found the light switch.

Blair looked at the bound and gagged figure of Hamish Macbeth.

He stooped over him and savagely ripped the gag from his mouth. "You're in deep shit, man," he said. "You're going to have to explain why you decided to do this on your own and why you withheld information."

It was a long, long day for Hamish Macbeth. He had to type out reports to explain why he had decided to investigate on his own. He learned that The Scotsman Hotel had been raided and all the bottles removed from the bar. Macbean had been ar-rested and charged with supplying illegal liquor to his cus-tomers and had been bailed to appear at the sheriff's court in Strathbane in a month's time.

Blair tried to make as much trouble for Hamish as possible,

but Superintendent Peter Daviot had said with irritating mildness that they would probably have never got on to it were it not for Hamish's unorthodox investigations. Hamish had not broken into the property. The door of the shed had been unlocked.

So Hamish was finally free to go. Blair's parting shot was that there was no police car available to take Hamish to Lochdubh and so he could walk. The last buses had gone by the time Hamish left police headquarters. He stood miserably out on the Lochdubh road, trying to hitch a lift. But cars which might have stopped for a policeman in uniform were not going to stop for a tired, unshaven man in black sweater and trousers.

Then just when he had given up hope of ever getting back to Lochdubh that night, the Currie sisters drew up beside him in their battered little Renault.

"You were on the six o'clock news," said Nessie as she drove off.

"It's getting like Chicago—Chicago," put in the repetitive Jessie.

Hamish dozed in the back seat until they drew up outside the police station. He blinked awake. "Someone's there," he said. "The lights are burning."

"It'll be that girlfriend of yours," sniffed Nessie.

Hamish walked into the police station. Sarah was sitting at the kitchen table.

"How did you get in?"

"I found the key under the doormat," said Sarah. "I'm glad you're safe. I heard about it on the news."

"I'll just see to the hens and sheep."

"The sheep have had their winter feed and the hens are locked up for the night," said Sarah. She added, seeing the look of surprise on his face, "My father is a farmer in Shropshire."

"I know little about you." Hamish sat down wearily at the

table. "I gather it was you who called police headquarters. They planned to drop me in a peat bog. They were running a big operation. The police have been raiding hotels and bars all over the place. The owners of The Drouthy Crofter in Braikie have been charged along with a lot of others."

"Well, now you're home safe, I'll be off," said Sarah.

"Won't you stay a bit?"

"No, you look exhausted. There's a casserole for you in the oven."

She stood up. He went to kiss her but she brushed past him, her head ducked.

"Sarah!" he called. But the closing of his kitchen door was the only answer he got.

The next day was as cold as iron. The birds were silent. Hoar frost glittered on the grass and on the branches of trees. Ice glittered in puddles. Outside the police station, the loch lay flat like glass.

It seemed a cold, friendless world where romance had died.

Hamish decided he'd had enough. His ribs hurt where he had been kicked and there was a sore red patch about his mouth from the gag. It was up to Strathbane with all their forensic resources, computers and reports to solve this case. He had been neglecting his domestic duties about the croft. He cleaned the police station thoroughly and then went out and fed his sheep. Towser's grave lay on the hill above the police station, a sad and silent reminder to one lonely policeman that even the dog who had loved him was no longer alive. By ten o'clock, he was beginning to feel considerably better because of all the physical exercise. He felt at peace. Deciding to leave the case alone had been a good idea.

The phone in the police station rang. Sarah was the first person he thought of. He thought it was her voice when he answered the phone and it took him a few moments to realise that the caller was Priscilla Halburton-Smythe.

"I've been waiting for a call from either you or Sarah," said Priscilla, "and I've been reading accounts of the death of this dentist."

Hamish sat down at his desk. "It's like this Priscilla, I've given up."

"That's not like you. Tell me all about it."

He began at the beginning with the murder and burglary and went on until he finished with his capture by the Smiley brothers.

"I'm sure you're feeling rattled, tired and fed up," said Priscilla sympathetically. "But what you used to do when you were stuck was to dig into the background of all the suspects. The answer, you always said, lay in the past. Also, Gilchrist was in debt and Gilchrist liked money. Could he have been involved with the Smiley brothers?"

"I'd thought of that," said Hamish slowly, "but I can't find any connection there."

"It certainly must have been a magnificent obsession that Maggie Bane had for Gilchrist."

"She was in love with him, yes, but why do you call it an obsession?"

"She gets a good degree, and by your account, apart from her ugly voice, she is very attractive. It must have been an obsession to make her bury herself alive in a dreary Highland town with a philanderer. Was there some jealous lover she left behind in St. Andrews? Might be worth finding out. You could start with one of her tutors."

"It's a long way to St. Andrews, Priscilla, and in this weather."

"You could phone."

He sighed. "No, no, I have always found it better to go in

person. I'll phone Strathbane. I'm supposed to be on leave for a couple of days anyway."

"Good hunting, Hamish. Phone me back if there's any result."

"Aye, I'll do that. Any hope of you coming back up here?"

"I'll be home for Christmas."

He wanted to ask, "Alone?" But what if she said no, she was bringing a friend with her, a male friend. Right at that moment, he didn't want to hear any more bad news.

Promising to phone, he said goodbye. He decided not to wear his uniform, he was not officially on duty. He phoned Strathbane and told them he was feeling unwell after his experience and would take two days leave. He then phoned Sergeant Macgregor at Cnothan and asked him to cover his beat for him.

He then locked up the police station after pinning a note on the door referring all callers to Cnothan.

As he drove out past the Tommel Castle Hotel, he resisted an impulse to swing the wheel, call at the hotel and see if Sarah would like to go with him.

Although the sky was threatening, no snow fell, and when he finally reached St. Andrews University, a gleam of pale sunlight was gilding the old university buildings.

It took some time to run Maggie Bane's former physics tutor to earth, but Hamish finally found himself sitting in the living room of a comfortable book-lined home, facing a Mr. James Packer, a surprisingly youthful and cherubic-looking man.

"I read about the case in the newspapers, of course," said Mr. Packer when Hamish explained the reason for his visit. "Do you know I was not very surprised that he had been killed."

"You knew him?" Hamish leaned forward eagerly.

"I knew of him. Maggie was a brilliant student. I thought it was that brilliance which isolated her from the other students.

She kept herself very much to herself. Didn't go much to parties and dances, didn't seem to have any boyfriends. Then right after the exams, I heard a rumour she had gone off to Paris with a middle-aged married man. I was concerned. On her return, I sent for her and told her bluntly I had heard the rumours. She laughed and said it was all respectable and that he was divorced and that they were going to get married, and until the wedding, she would work for him at his practise in Braikie. I counselled her that she was too young to know her own mind and that she was throwing away a brilliant future but she was so obviously very much in love."

There was a sad little silence. Then Mr. Packer said, "But he did not marry her, did he?"

"No," said Hamish, "and it appears he was not very faithful to her either. Apart from being a brilliant student, tell me more about Maggie Bane."

"To tell the truth, I was amazed by her passion for this dentist. I always thought of her as being rather cold and analytical. I thought she did not mix with the other students because she despised them, rather than out of shyness."

"What is her background?"

"Doting mother and father, possibly no longer doting. I heard the mother used to call at the university with home-baked cakes and things like that for Maggie, and Maggie was quite dreadfully rude to her. I suppose, you know, I really only saw Maggie's intellectual brilliance. But looking back, I don't suppose Maggie Bane was a very nice character."

"Do you think she could be violent?"

"I do not know. I would not have credited her with violence, but until the advent of Gilchrist, I would not have thought her capable of passion either."

"I wish I'd known Gilchrist," said Hamish. "I only saw him dead. He was nothing much to look at—white hair, white face—typical dentist, in fact. There must have been something in his character to attract women. He liked the high life and he left a lot of debt."

Mr. Packer gave an odd little nod of his head as if Hamish had just confirmed something he had already thought. "Have you noticed, Mr. Macbeth, those ugly little millionaires who usually have some gorgeous blonde hanging on their arm? Women find an ambience of power and money almost irresistible. And before you damn me as being a chauvinist and politically incorrect, I mean some women. This is not Palm Beach, this is the north of Scotland where things are scaled down. A man who drives a large car and offers trips to Paris just like that must have struck Maggie Bane as a rare exotic. I think she is much to be pitied. I think I shall write to her if you would be so good as to furnish me with her address. I think she could channel all that passion and energy into a successful career."

Hamish took out his notebook, wrote down Maggie's address, and passed it over.

"There's something else I want to ask you—about nicotine poison."

"It's very easy to make."

"You will see from the newspapers, an illegal still was raided. I thought that might have been used. I mean anyone with the machinery to manufacture illegal whisky would be able to make nicotine poison."

"I should think any bright schoolchild might be able to do the same in a school lab."

Hamish sighed. "Motive, that's the thing."

"It's usually drunkenness, love or money."

"There was this robbery at The Scotsman Hotel. I kept thinking that Gilchrist with his love of spending and being low on funds might have had something to do with it. I mean, Mrs.

Macbean, that's the manager's wife, might have let something slip about the money, about the safe having a wooden back."

"Or," said Mr. Packer, crossing a neat pair of ankles in Argyll socks, "if he was such a charmer, he could have worked on her. Surely such an enormous sum of money for a bingo prize would be advertised by the hotel in the newspapers."

"Yes, it was."

"This is *fun*," said the tutor happily. "I feel quite like Dr. Watson. Tell me about this Mrs. Macbean."

"She isn't a looker, middle-aged, waspish, hair in curlers from morning till night. Husband is said to beat her up, but she does not seem afraid of him. Told a friend of mine"—oh, Sarah, what happened to us?—"that a woman with a bread-knife in her hand didn't need to be afraid of any man. Said she put laxative in his morning coffee after he had beaten her and threatened it would be poison the next time."

"Mrs. Macbean sounds a likely candidate."

"But she would need help. Someone with strength and coldness murdered Gilchrist and hoisted him into the dentist's chair and drilled all his teeth."

"You came here," said Mr. Packer, "to find out more about Maggie Bane. I assume this is because there is often something in the person's past which will highlight some murderous side of their character?"

"That is often the case."

"Then perhaps you should try to find out a bit more about what Mrs. Macbean is like?"

"You're right. I might just call down to Leith and see what I can find."

Blessing the motorways which made travel so easy, Hamish drove down to Edinburgh and so to Leith. He had fortunately a note of Mrs. Macbean's original address in his notebook.

There might be someone living there or living close by who might remember her.

The early Scottish night had fallen when he finally entered a Georgian tenement in Leith. The woman who answered the door to him said that, yes, the police had already been round asking questions but she had never known the woman. Try Mrs. Morton on the ground floor.

Mrs. Morton turned out to be God's gift to a policeman—a lonely grey-haired widow anxious for company and anxious to talk.

"Yes, yes, I remember Agnes Macwhirter. Beautiful girl and knew it. Full of herself. All the boys were mad for her. Said she was going to be someone someday. Went to business college and said she would be secretary to someone famous, like a film star."

"And did she become secretary to someone famous?"

"No, she ended up as a pretty ordinary secretary working for the manager of a children's wear factory in Dumfries."

Hamish looked at her sharply. "Did you say Dumfries?"

"Yes, indeed. Now what was the place called. I'll remember in a moment. It's funny at my age how one remembers things clearly from the old days but nothing much about yesterday. I remember her mother coming down to tell me. Poor Mrs. Macwhirter, the cancer took her off. I know, it was Tot Modes, that's it, Tot Modes in Dumfries."

"Can you remember the name of the manager?"

She shook her head regretfully.

Dumfries, thought Hamish. That's where Gilchrist had come from.

"I'd best find somewhere to stay the night and then I might drive over to Dumfries in the morning."

"I have a spare room here," said Mrs. Morton, loneliness peering out of her old eyes. "I would be glad of the company."

Hamish hesitated. He would have liked to rack up in some anonymous hotel room and sort out his thoughts. But he knew what it was like to feel lonely and one day he would be old himself, and to hell with it . . .

"That is most kind of you," he said. He retired early however, feeling if he looked through another album of ancient photographs he would scream.

He awoke early but Mrs. Morton was up before him and had prepared a massive breakfast. Hamish longed to offer to pay for food and accommodation but was afraid of offending her. But when he left, he put two twenty-pound notes in an envelope and left it on the bedside table with a note: "This is for your favourite charity," hoping that Mrs. Morton's favourite charity was herself, for he knew she sorely needed money. The little flat was spotless, but everything was shabby and worn.

He set out for Dumfries, grateful that although the weather was cold, it was still dry. Skeletal winter trees held their black tracery of branches up in supplication to an unforgiving sky. He took all seasons as they came, finding some beauty in all, but beginning to have an intimation of how much he would learn to hate the winter when he was older. Mrs. Morton had said she hailed each spring as a gift from God, knowing she would be alive for another year, because old people died in winter.

He had not phoned, and wondering if the children's clothing factory would be still in operation, he stopped at the main post office in Dumfries and looked up the phone book. To his relief Tot Modes was listed. He drove out to an industrial estate and found the factory, which consisted of two long low buildings and asked for the manager.

The manager, a Mr. Goodman, was, Hamish saw with disappointment, a relatively young man. But he explained why he had called.

"That would be in my father's time," said Mr. Goodman.

"Is he still alive?"

"Yes, I'll just phone him and say you will be calling, and then I'll give you directions."

Another twenty minutes and Hamish found himself confronting Mr. Goodman, senior, a portly old gentleman with a round face covered in so many broken veins it looked like a relief map. His eyes had the watery sheen of the perpetual drinker, but he was sober that morning and seemed delighted to have company.

"Agnes Macwhirter," he said. "Aye, I remember her well. Bonnie lassie."

"Can you tell me what she was like?"

"Very good secretary. Miss Perfect. Tailored white blouses, pencil skirts, that sort of thing. Walking out with a respectable young doctor."

"Doctor?" Hamish looked disappointed. "I was hoping to find some connection between her and that dentist who's just been murdered, Frederick Gilchrist."

"Oh, him." Then the old man stared at Hamish. "Of course, Gilchrist, that was the fellow. He was only a student when he was here. That's right. Someone said he was a dental student, studying to be a dentist."

"And he knew Miss Macwhirter?"

"Knew her? He ruined that lassie's life."

"How?"

"At first it seemed the Romeo and Juliet romance o' all time. He would wait outside the factory for her in his car every evening. She was besotted with him. I got a wee bit worried because her work began to fall off, and then she began to turn up late in the mornings, hungover and—what's the word?—looking shagged."

Hamish suppressed a grin. "You mean they were having an affair?"

"Aye, talk went around. I couldn't understand why the time passed on his holidays with no sign of a ring on her finger. I mean, things were stricter in those days. Her work got worse. I sat her down and had a wee talk to her. I said unless she pulled her socks up, I would need to fire her. She had grown insolent and she tossed her hair and said she'd soon be married so I had better start looking for a replacement, and then the next day she didn't turn up, and a week later, she sent a note saying she had resigned. I got another secretary and forgot about it, until, oh, it must have been three months later, I was walking along with the wife, and she said, 'Let's cross the road. There's these awful bikers.' I looked and there was this gang of blokes on motorcycles outside this pub, all sideburns and black leather and metal studs, and hanging around the neck of one of the bikers was Agnes Macwhirter. What a change! Her hair was a brassy blonde and she looked like a tart. I thought, that one will be on the streets before long, but she married one of those hoodlums, called Macbean, I think. He subsequently ran a pub and then a hotel, and then I never heard any more of her, Macbean or Gilchrist. The odd thing was that I read all about the murder in the newspapers and I didn't connect the Gilchrist who was murdered with the dental student. I don't get out much and no one comes to see me. Will you be having a dram?"

"I'm driving," said Hamish.

"Well, a cup of tea?"

He wanted to escape from the loneliness of the old, but he said, "Thank you," and virtue had its reward, for after making tea, Mr. Goodman produced some old staff photos. "There's Agnes, at the Christmas party."

She had indeed been beautiful then, and with a voluptuous figure.

Here was a motive for murder at last, thought Hamish. He forced himself to spend an hour with Mr. Goodman and then made his escape, putting on the police siren this time and breaking all speed limits on the road north.

When he finally reached Lochdubh at seven in the evening, he went straight to the police station and reluctantly picked up the phone. He knew if he tried to question Mrs. Macbean himself, he would probably be thrown out of the hotel, and this was news he could not, should not keep to himself.

He told Jimmy Anderson what he had found out. "You're a miracle, Hamish," said Jimmy. "I'll tell Blair and we'll pull her in now."

"You can tell him, I want to be in on the questioning," said Hamish. "He would never have found this out without me."

"Aye, I'll tell him. Give us a bit to get her back here."

Hamish then phoned Sarah but was told she had gone out for dinner. He went along to the Italian restaurant, but she was not there, so he ate a solitary meal and then set out for Strathbane.

Mrs. Macbean had red plastic hair rollers in this time. Hamish sat in a corner of the interrogation room with a policewoman while Blair began the examination.

"Why did you not tell us you knew Gilchrist afore you were married?"

"It was a long time ago," she said angrily.

"You had an affair with him. Did you murder him?"

"No, I did not," she said, folding her arms. "The only reason I went to him was because he pulled my teeth and didnae charge a thing."

Hamish looking at her thin mouth, rollered hair, bad-tempered face, thick body and rounded shoulders could not find a trace left of that happy, laughing beautiful girl of the staff photograph.

"Where were you on the morning of the murder?"

"I was at the hotel."

"Witnesses?"

"I was in my room. My daughter'll tell ye."

"We need an independent witness. One of the guests, someone like that."

"Whit time was the murder?"

"Between ten and eleven as you very well know," said Blair.

"Aye, I was at the hotel. I know. I phoned down to Johnny at the bar sometime about then and asked if the insurance men had been yet."

"We'll check with him. But I think you killed him," Blair shouted right in her face.

She leaned back in her chair and looked at him with contempt. "Prove it."

The questioning went on while Hamish studied her, his mind working furiously. He was suddenly sure she had not done it. But she had known Gilchrist, had loved him passionately. Jeannie Gilchrist had thought her husband had been married before because she sensed there was someone in his past he had not got over. Yet Gilchrist with his penchant for attractive young women would find nothing left in her to love, in what had become an ugly, bad-tempered woman. She could not even pay him to . . . He sat up. It was a long shot.

Hamish interrupted Blair. "Sir?"

Blair swung round furiously. "Whit?"

"I chust wanted to ask Mrs. Macbean where the money is, the money she promised to Gilchrist."

There was a dead silence. One red roller fell from Mrs. Macbean's head and came to rest in front of Blair.

Mrs. Macbean was now staring at Hamish, all truculence gone.

"The way I see it is this." Hamish's gentle Highland voice sounded in the stillness of the room. "You had loved Gilchrist more than you had ever loved any man. You are unhappy in your marriage. You could no longer attract him. He was having an affair with a pretty young girl. But he liked money, he was worried sick about money. I think for two hundred and fifty thousand pounds he would have gone off with you. What happened? Did he take the money and then refuse?" Hamish watched her face closely. "No, that's not it. You've still got the money. You'd best tell us where for we'll take your room apart, take the hotel apart. I know you've got it and we'll keep you here for as long as it takes to get you to confess."

A long silence followed. Blair gave an impatient grunt. For one moment, he thought Hamish had discovered something, but this was sidetracking. He wanted a murderer.

"Better to be damned as a thief than a murderer," said Hamish.

But she had regained her composure. She shrugged. "Search my room all you want," she said. "You won't find anything."

Hamish stared at her. "No," he said, "perhaps not in your room. Your daughter's room?" No reaction. "So somewhere in the hotel." She stared at him boldly. "Och, well, now let's chust say not in the hotel, but outside . . . buried."

Her eyes flickered. "Can I have a cigarette?"

"Buried," said Hamish flatly. "In the hotel grounds. Should be easy to find this winter weather. We'll look for a sign of recent digging. Shouldn't take long."

Silence.

"Well, you've had your say, Hamish . . ." Blair was just beginning when Mrs. Macbean, who had not taken her eyes off

Hamish, said, "You bastard. You knew all the time. Who was it told you? Darleen?"

"So it was you what stole the money," said Blair, suddenly wishing Hamish miles away so that he could take all the credit for this.

She gave a little sigh. "I loved him," she said. She looked at Hamish and for a moment her eyes blazed with something, for one split second the ghost of the pretty girl she had once been shone out at him, and then she began to sob in a helpless dreary way. "I couldn't even mourn him," she said at last. "I couldnae even shed a tear or folks might have guessed. He said if I got the money we could go away together and start a new life. It wisnae really stealing, that's what he said. The insurance company would pay up and the insurance company could afford it. We would go to Spain. I would get away from Macbean. Funny thing, marriage. I think I hated that man a week after we were wed but the years dragged on and on and on. I stayed for Darleen, but she's become a hard little bitch. She wouldnae hae missed me. Oh God, I didnae kill him."

But Blair gave her a wolfish smile and hitched his chair closer to the table. As far as he was concerned, Mrs. Macbean had killed Gilchrist and he was going to stay up all night to make her confess.

Hamish arrived back at the police station in Lochdubh at dawn, feeling bone weary. Despite Blair's insistent and truculent questioning, Mrs. Macbean had not cracked. She had told them where the money was hidden and it had been recovered but she insisted she had not murdered the dentist. The barman was pulled in and confirmed that she had phoned down at the time the murder was taking place. And then he remembered a maid had taken clean sheets up to Mrs. Macbean's room. Mrs. Macbean did not share a room with her husband. Both lived separately in respective hotel rooms. A long wait while the maid was located, a local woman with an impeccable reputation, a Mrs. Tandy, who confirmed that at ten-thirty on the morning of the murder, she had taken clean sheets in to Mrs. Macbean. So that had been that. Mrs. Macbean had been charged with the theft. The fact that Hamish Macbeth had solved the robbery did not earn him any kudos with Blair, who had grown quite savage when he had realised the murder was still unsolved.

Hamish went wearily to bed. Before he fell asleep, he wondered again if there had been any connection between the Smiley brothers and the dentist. Greed for money had been at the back of the Smileys' operation and Gilchrist had been greedy for money.

The phone rang several times from the police office, dragging him up out of the depths of sleep, but each time he remembered he had left the answering machine switched on and the murderer was hardly likely to phone him up and confess.

He slept for six hours and rose, still feeling tired and gritty. He washed and shaved and put on his uniform. Then he went into the police office and played back the messages on the answering machine. First Sergeant Macgregor from Cnothan's cross voice, wondering whether Hamish was back on duty, then Mrs. Wellington asking whether she should go back and instruct Kylie and her friends further in the paths of righteousness, and then a lilting voice, saying cautiously, "This is Fred Sutherland. I think I've found out something about Kylie. I should've told you afore, but I didnae think of it. Can ye come as soon as possible?"

CHAPTER NINE

Alice was puzzled. "In our country," she remarked, "there's only one day at a time."

—Lewis Carroll

As he drove to Braikie, Hamish wondered what Fred Sutherland had to tell him. Whatever Fred had to tell him about Kylie was probably something he knew already.

There is very little daylight in the north of Scotland in winter and Hamish, still tired, still with sore ribs, felt he had been living in a long dark tunnel for some time.

He parked outside the dress shop. Slowly he mounted the stairs, past the dentist's surgery. He then realised he had been making his way up the stone staircase by the light of the street lamp outside. There was no light on the staircase. He went down to the surgery door and looked up. The lightbulb on the socket on the first landing was not there.

He went back to the Land Rover and got his torch and began to climb the stairs again. His senses were alert now, listening for any movement, any sound, as wary of danger as an animal in the woods.

He knocked at Fred Sutherland's door. Then he flashed the torch upwards. No bulb in the light socket here either.

He tried the handle. The door swung slowly open. "Fred," called Hamish. "Fred Sutherland?"

Was this another trick by Kylie and her friends? But then old Fred would never be a party to it.

He found the light switch and pressed it down. The little entrance hall was bleak and bare.

He then went into the living room. Fred Sutherland lay dead on the floor, his head bashed in. Someone had struck him a cruel and savage blow on the forehead.

Hamish knelt down by the old man and felt for the pulse which he knew already he would not find. His first guilty and miserable thought was that this was what became of involving the public in a murder enquiry. He saw the phone on a little table by the fireplace and went and lifted the receiver. The phone was dead. He looked down at the cord and saw that it had been cut near the wall.

He darted down the stairs to the Land Rover and contacted Strathbane on the radio and then, that done, went back up the stairs to wait. Without touching anything, he studied the scene. There was no sign of forced entry. The television set was still there. No drawers had been ransacked. It looked as if Fred had not kept the outside door locked. Someone had walked in and bludgeoned him to death in the doorway of his living room. Hamish then looked sadly at the old framed photographs dotted about the room: Fred, handsome and gallant in army uniform, Fred with a pretty girl on his arm, then a wedding photograph.

The contingent from Strathbane finally arrived, headed by Detective Chief Inspector Blair, red-eyed and truculent, with pyjama bottoms peeking out from below his trousers, showing he had been roused from bed.

Hamish told Blair about the message from the old man. "Right," snapped Blair, "let's get this girl in for questioning. Why didn't you tell us about her before, Macbeth?"

"I had only just found out," lied Hamish. "I have a report typed up I was going to send over to you tomorrow."

Blair looked at him suspiciously. "Your trouble, Macbeth, is that you like to keep everything to yourself. If I find you caused this old boy's death by not reporting what you know about this girl to us in due time, I'll have ye off the force."

Hamish gave him Kylie's address. He was sure she would not tell about the entrapment—unless of course she panicked when the police arrived and assumed that was why they were there.

When two detectives and a policewoman had been dispatched to Kylie's address, Blair turned again to Hamish. "So what was in this mysterious report o' yours about this girl?"

"There was nothing much," said Hamish. "She'd been out on a date with Gilchrist and he made a pass at her. She threatened to tell everyone about it and he promised to buy her a car. A month passed. No car. When she approached him, he told her no one would believe her."

"You should have phoned all that in right away," howled Blair. "God protect me from daft, stupid Highland policemen!" Blair hailed from Glasgow. But guilt-ridden Hamish was not going to tell his superior officer that he had requested Fred to ask about and find out what he could about Kylie.

He asked if he should be at Strathbane for the questioning of Kylie Fraser, and Blair grunted, "We'll see. Where does she work."

"In the chemists along the street."

"We'd best be having a word with her boss. What's his name?"

Hamish remembered going into the shop, remembered the small fussy man. What had Kylie called him? "Cody," he said suddenly. "Mr. Cody."

"Well, to save you hanging around here, find out where Cody lives and get yourself over there."

"But Kylie Fraser . . . ?"

"Och, I think we'll do just fine withoot the great brain o' Hamish Macbeth. And how many times do I have tae tell ye tae address me as 'sir'?"

Hamish looked up Mr. Cody's home address in the telephone book and took himself off. He was tortured with pictures of poor dead Fred Sutherland who would still be alive if one daft policeman had not asked him to investigate a murder.

Mr. Cody lived in a trim bungalow called Our House on the edge of the town. Hamish glanced at his watch. It was only ten at night. It seemed as if a lifetime had passed since he had left Lochdubh that evening.

He rang the doorbell and waited. It was answered by a rigidly corseted woman. He wondered vaguely why women in the north of Scotland still squeezed themselves into old-fashioned corsets while their fat sisters of the south let it all hang out.

"What's happened?" she cried when she saw Hamish's uniformed figure.

"I am just here to have a word with Mr. Cody."

"What about? Is it his sister? Is it bad news?"

"No, no," said Hamish soothingly. "Just part of our investigations."

"You'd better come in. Charles! It's the police for you."

The small, fussy-looking man Hamish had seen first in the chemists came down the stairs. He had grey hair neatly combed back, round glasses and a small mouth. He was wearing a fawn cardigan over a shirt collar and tie and grey trousers and highly polished black shoes.

"How can I be of help to you, officer?" he asked. "We'll go into the lounge. I hope the shop has not been broken into."

"No," said Hamish. He followed him into an overfurnished room and took off his cap.

"Mr. Fred Sutherland has been found dead, murdered."

Mr. Cody looked startled. "Who is he?"

Hamish thought suddenly of the little table in the living room on which the phone rested in Fred's flat. There had been a small array of medicine bottles beside the phone.

"He lived above the dentist, Gilchrist."

"But this is terrible . . . terrible. Who would do such a thing? And why ask me?"

"It concerns your assistant, Kylie Fraser. Mr. Sutherland left a message on my answering machine this evening, saying he had found something out about her and asking me to call. Detectives are questioning Kylie. Can you think what it might have been that he found out?"

Mrs. Cody was sitting across from them. "I told you and told you to get rid of that flighty piece," she said. "She hangs about with some of the worst elements in the town."

The pharmacist ignored his wife. "I had no trouble with her in the shop. I know she has a bit of a reputation, but during working hours, she's pleasant and hard-working and the customers like her. She sells quite a lot of cosmetics for me."

"And wears most of them all at once on her stupid face," said his wife waspishly.

"Say Mr. Sutherland had really found out something about her, someone didn't want us to know about," said Hamish, "have you any idea who that someone would be?"

He shook his head. "I really don't know." A little wire-haired dachshund appeared from behind the sofa, went to Hamish and pressed its small shivering body against his legs. He leaned down to pat it.

"Just in the line of enquiry, can you tell me where you were this evening?"

"What time?"

"Say between eight o'clock and half past nine."

"I had a coffee with my wife and we watched a quiz programme on television and then I took Suky out for his usual evening walk."

"Where did you go?"

"Just up to Brady's field at the end of the houses. Suky likes to run about the field looking for rabbits. He disappeared for quite a time and I had the devil of a job getting him back."

"I thought Suky was a girl's name," said Hamish.

"Oh, well, we call him that," said the pharmacist, pressing his hands together. "This has been a great shock. I did not know the man . . . what was his name?"

"Sutherland. Fred Sutherland. There is no other pharmacist in Braikie, surely."

"No, I'm the only one."

"I noticed Mr. Sutherland had several medicine bottles in his flat. I am sure if I go back and look at the labels, I will find the name of your shop on them."

Mr. Cody coloured up. "You are making me feel guilty when I have no reason to feel guilty. Kylie hands me prescriptions and I make up the bottles and pills and paste labels on them. I cannot remember every name."

"But a resident of Braikie who had probably been going to you for years!"

"I am afraid my memory is not what it was."

"So there is nothing more you can tell us about Kylie? She did not confide in you?"

"No, of course not. We were employer and employee. She would hardly giggle to me about her boyfriends."

"Did you know she had gone out with Gilchrist? That she claims he came on to her and that he slapped her face? She threatened to tell everyone and he said if she kept quiet he would buy her a car. But he subsequently told her that since it was her word against his, everyone would believe him."

"This is what comes of employing a girl like that," said Mrs. Cody. "She's not our sort. This is what comes, Charles, from associating with a low-life creature like that."

"It is very hard to get staff," said Mr. Cody furiously. "Kylie has stayed longer than anyone else. The young people here prefer to stay on the dole and do a bit of moonlighting. I am sorry I cannot help you further, officer, but I know very little about Kylie."

"I must warn you that you will be subjected to more questioning," said Hamish.

He said goodbye to them and then drove as fast as he could to Strathbane. He was anxious to sit in on the questioning of Kylie.

He was lucky in that the detectives sent to get her had not found her at home and had finally run her to earth in the pub and that Blair had radioed them by that time with instructions not to say anything to her. Ignoring a filthy look from Blair, he took a chair in the corner of the interrogation room, just in time to hear Kylie, who was fed on a regular diet of American movies, plead the Fifth Amendment.

"This is Scotland," growled Blair, "and no' Chicago."

"What's it about?" asked Kylie, her eyes flickering to where Hamish sat in the corner.

"Fred Sutherland has been murdered."

"What! Thon auld fellow what lived above Gilchrist?" Her face went white under her makeup. "What's that to do wi' me?"

"Mr. Sutherland left a message on PC Macbeth's answering

machine tonight, saying that he had found out something about you. When PC Macbeth went to see him, he found he had been brutally murdered."

"But I was in the pub all evening. Ask anyone. Ask the barman."

"We will. But we hae a fair idea what it was that Sutherland wanted tae tell Macbeth. You had a fling wi' Gilchrist."

He shouted this last accusation in her face.

To Hamish's surprise, the colour began to come back into Kylie's cheeks. She gave a resigned little shrug. "Well, you knew about that." She jerked her head in Hamish's direction. "He knew about that."

Blair took her all through her date with Gilchrist, about the promise of the car. He accused her of having got some of the young hoodlums she hung out with to murder the dentist. He ranted and raved, but Kylie remained immovable. She had a cast-iron alibi for the whole evening and that was that. Sutherland had probably found out about her going down to Inverness with Gilchrist and that was what he wanted to tell Hamish. Why he had been murdered, she had no idea. It was up to them to find out who did it. In fact as the wearisome questioning continued, Kylie became more relaxed as Blair became more furious and frustrated.

At last she was warned to keep herself in readiness for more questioning and a policewoman was told to escort her back to Braikie.

Hamish went wearily back to Lochdubh to type up his reports—first the one on Kylie and Gilchrist which he had said he had already done, and then of his interview with Mr. Cody.

He finally went to bed and fell asleep and dreamed guilty dreams of a dead Fred Sutherland reaching up from an open grave and crying, "You could have saved me. It's all your fault, Hamish Macbeth."

His first thought the next morning was that he should start off at the Old Timers Club that Fred had talked about. He had said he would ask questions there. Perhaps he had a particular friend he had confided in.

His heart was heavy as he took the road to Braikie. He stopped abruptly outside the road leading up to the Smiley brothers' croft. A troll-like figure was repairing the fencing. He got down and walked up, wondering if Blair had gone mad and released the brothers.

But as he drew closer, he saw the man was neither Pete nor Stourie but of similar build and appearance and just as hairy.

"Who are you?" asked Hamish.

The man glowered at him. "I'm Jock Smiley, their cousin. Are you the bastard what put them away?"

"Me and others," said Hamish, "and they were prepared to murder me."

"They neffer harmed a fly in their lives. All they did was make a wee bit o' whisky which is every Highlandman's right."

"Oh, come on. Pull the other one. They had a major business. This was the bootlegging on a grand scale."

"It's got nothing to do with me anyway," said Jock. "Bugger off."

Hamish walked back to the Land Rover. What a pity there had not been proof that the Smileys had killed Gilchrist. They were the only suspects who had the strength, character and expertise to do it.

The Old Timers Club was in a smart new community centre opened, said a plaque on the front, by Princess Anne in 1991. Marvelling not for the first time at the energy of the Princess Royal, Hamish pushed open the door and went in.

Various people were sitting around, watching television, playing cards, or gossiping.

An elderly woman came forward to meet him. "Can I help you, officer?"

"I would like to talk to someone who knew Fred Sutherland well."

"Oh, poor Fred. That's young people for you these days. They would kill a man for twopence."

Hamish reflected that as far as anyone had been able to judge, nothing had been stolen from Fred's flat.

"But Mr. Tam Carmichael was a great friend of Fred's," she went on.

"Is he here?"

"No, it's a wee bit early for Tam. But I can give you his address. He lives above the bakers just along from the chemists in the main street."

Hamish thanked her and left. He walked along to the bakers and up a stone staircase at the side of the shop. MR. T. CARMICHAEL was on a neat name plate outside the door of a first floor flat. He knocked and waited. A little gnome of a man answered the door wearing a dressing gown over striped pyjamas. Tufts of grey hair stuck up on his head. His nose was very large and his eyes very small and sharp.

"You've come about Fred," he said heavily. "Come in. You're Macbeth."

Hamish followed him into a cosy little living room where a coal fire blazed on the hearth.

They both sat down. "Last night," began Hamish, "Mr. Sutherland left a message on my answering machine saying he had found out something about Kylie Fraser and then he was murdered. Did he tell you what it was?"

Old Tam shook his head. "He was that excited, I can tell you that. He fancied himself as Inspector Poirot. Questions, questions, questions. He was so proud you had told him to help."

"I think I helped to kill him," said Hamish miserably.

The sharp old eyes looked at his distressed face. "Now, then, laddie," said Tam, "don't be getting yourself in a bind. We've all got to go sometime. Fred was so happy and interested and he'd been gloomy and distressed of late. He smoked about eighty a day and I don't think he would have kept his health much longer. I'll miss him. There's not that many men around the club. It's aye the ladies who outlast us. So that made the pair of us great favourites. An interest in the ladies is something you dinnae lose with age although you can do damn all about it."

"Was there any particular lady he was friendly with?" asked Hamish.

"Aye, Annie Taine. She'll be in a sore state over his death."

"And where does she live?"

"She's got a wee bit o' a croft house out near Mrs. Harrison, her what was soft about Gilchrist. It's called Dunroamin, right on the road. You can't miss it."

"I wonder why Mr. Sutherland didn't tell you what it was he found out," said Hamish.

"All he said was, 'I think I'm on to something, Tam, but I'll let you know after I've had a word with that policeman.' I'm telling ye, he had the time of his life."

Hamish stood up. "I only wish he were still alive. I think I'll have this on my conscience till the end of time."

Tam put one old gnarled hand on a large Bible on the table next to him. "You cannae criticise the ways o' the Lord. If Fred had been meant to live, then he would have lived on. I gather he was hit on the head."

"Yes, I should think he died instantly."

"Look at it this way, a short sharp death was a kinder way for old Fred to go than coughing out his life."

Hamish thanked him and left. As he drove out on the road to where Annie Taine lived, he thought again about Mrs. Harrison. Perhaps he should see her again. But he went straight to the cottage called Dunroamin first.

Mrs. Annie Taine was a well-preserved seventy-something with hair of an improbable blonde. Her eyes were red with weeping. "Poor Fred," she said when she saw Hamish. "What a dreadful thing to happen."

She invited Hamish in. How independent these old people were, thought Hamish, the ones who managed to keep fit enough to manage a home of their own. Everything in her little living room was neat and sparkling.

"I have just come from Mr. Tam Carmichael," began Hamish, "and he told me you were a particular friend of Mr. Sutherland. He was interested in the death of Mr. Gilchrist and I gather he was asking questions. He left a message for me last night to say he had found out something about Kylie Fraser. Did he tell you what that something was?"

She shook her head. "He was so excited. I think he dreamed of standing up in court and giving evidence. He asked me to repair a small tear in his best suit for him because he said that would look grand in front of the television cameras. We didn't take him seriously. I suppose we all seem a bit gaga at times. And men are such little children. Always living in Walter Mitty dreams. Let me think. He did say something."

Hamish waited.

"He said, 'The things middle-aged men get up to wi' wee lassies, you'd never believe.'"

Hamish gave a little sigh. "I suppose he was talking about Gilchrist."

"You mean Mr. Gilchrist and Kylie. My!"

"He didn't get anywhere with her but I suppose Fred Sutherland found out and that's what he wanted to tell me."

"But don't you see," cried Annie, "that must have been the

reason Fred was killed! Kylie hangs out with some awful fellows at the pub."

"There was no reason for Kylie to worry. I already knew, you see, and she knew that."

She clasped her hands and looked at him beseechingly. "You must find out who did this wicked thing. Mr. Gilchrist was a nasty man and no one really mourns him, but everyone loved Fred."

"I'll do my best," said Hamish, "but if you find out anything or remember anything, please let me know."

She promised she would. He then went to Mrs. Harrison's but she was not at home. He then remembered he had asked Mrs. Edwardson of the dress shop to ask about Kylie as well and thought he had better warn her.

She was there as usual in her empty shop among the droopy dresses and china dummies with 1930 faces and improbable wigs.

"You don't need to worry about me," she said in answer to Hamish's warning. "I haven't been asking about although I did warn Kylie you'd been asking about her. I've got so much to do here, you see."

"Such as what?"

She bridled. "Serving customers, of course, making alterations, and taking inventory of the stock."

Hamish's Highland curiosity almost prompted him to ask her when she had last sold anything at all.

"So you haven't heard anything that might be of help to me?"

"Not really, and I do not see why I should do your job for you, Officer."

"I'll leave you to all your customers," said Hamish with a flash of Highland malice. "I'll chust be fighting my way to the door through them all."

He stood outside the shop, irresolute. Then he saw Jimmy Anderson loping down the street.

"Just the man," hailed Jimmy. "Let's go for a dram."

They walked in silence to The Drouthy Crofter. The bar was empty.

Hamish knew Jimmy had to be fueled up with whisky before he could get any information out of him and so he bought him a double and said, "Let's sit down over there. What's the latest. Was anything stolen from Fred Sutherland's flat?"

"No sign of it. He wasnae the type o' old boy to keep it under the bed either. How did you get on with Kylie's boss?"

"Not very far. He kept her on because she was a steady worker and the customers liked her. I see his point. The young people up here like to go on the dole and do a bit of moonlighting. They're hardly the workers o' the world. This is the second time someone has gone up that stair to commit murder and no one's seen anyone. Certainly the lights were out on the stair but there was a streetlight outside."

"I'll tell you something about Braikie," said Jimmy. "Has it ever dawned on you how dead it is, even in the middle o' the day? What am I talking about? Especially in the middle o' the day. Down south the supermarkets are open the whole time and some o' the Asian shops are open round-the-clock, but up here everything closes down as tight as a drum at lunchtime. Then any other wee town in Scotland, you'll aye see groups o' people standing about talking. Not here. It's as bad as that other hellhole, Cnothan. I've been watching. About nine in the morning, everyone goes to the shops, get what they want and disappear. By ten o'clock, the place is as dead as anything. Around five o'clock, just before the shops close, they all come out again. The young people spend their day in this pub after they awake about two in the afternoon, and the old people go to that club of theirs. A special bus goes round and collects them at nine in the morning. The middle-aged stay at home and watch the soaps. I'm telling you, Hamish, if I had to live in Braikie, I'd cut my wrists."

"What's happened to Kylie now?"

"Back at Strathbane for questioning. She's got a lawyer now."

"Who's she got?"

"Mr. Armstrong-Gulliver."

Hamish raised his eyebrows in surprise. "That'll cost her a pretty penny. How can she afford him, and where are her parents and who are her parents?"

"Mother. Single mother in Inverness. On the game. Hasn't seen Kylie for two years. Broken home. Violence."

"What do you make of Kylie?"

"Sexy little piece, but as hard as nails. I've seen strong men crumble before Blair. But not our Kylie."

Hamish leaned back in his chair. "If Gilchrist were still alive, I would be suspecting him o' the murder of Fred to keep the old man's mouth shut about him and Kylie. There's something verra obvious we're missing, Jimmy."

"The fact is," said Jimmy, "we're cluttered up wi' crime and suspects. There's that robbery at the hotel and Mrs. Macbean being an auld flame o' Gilchrist. There's the Smileys and their illegal still. You said they were going to drop you in a peat bog? Do that to a copper and you'll murder anyone."

"I don't know," said Hamish. "There's something about that mad couple that belongs to the Highlands long gone. I don't think mentally that they'd got as far as the nineteenth century let alone the twentieth."

Jimmy laughed. "They had all the twentieth-century equipment to make the hooch."

"Aye, but to them that was a Highlander's legitimate livelihood and a nosy policeman in their minds is the same as a visit from the redcoats in the eighteenth century. Into the bog with them."

"Sounds daft to me. Anyway, now Kylie's got her hotshot lawyer, Blair'll need to treat her with kid gloves. Ach, I'm sick o' the whole thing. The super says to Blair, 'Are you sure Hamish hasn't come up with something? He usually does,' and Blair oiled and crept and said, 'Yes sir, I'll ask him,' and then went down to the detectives room and took his temper out on all of us."

"Another drink?" asked Hamish.

"Aye, that would be grand."

As Hamish stood at the bar ordering the drinks, he noticed the pub was beginning to fill up. Perhaps he, Hamish Macbeth, had too free and easy an approach to law and order. He should have arrested Kylie for trying to entrap him in a rape scene, he should have arrested the seer for buying illegal whisky, or more likely, accepting it from the Smileys, he should have never gone to the Smileys' on his own that night. He felt he was the muddled, bumbling Highland idiot that Blair often claimed he was.

He took the drinks back to the table, aware of the hostility towards himself and Jimmy emanating from the other customers.

"Look at this lot," sneered Jimmy. "A good day's work would kill them."

Hamish kept his own thoughts. He thought that living on the state was a very seductive situation. Why would anyone want to go out to work when they didn't have to? The jobs in the Highlands, farmworkers, forestry men, ghillies and gamekeepers, were all too physical for a new generation brought up on alcohol and instant food. He envied Jimmy in a way for he often wished he was not able to see the other point of view.

"So to get back to the case," said Hamish, "I called on that old bat, Harrison, but she wasn't at home."

"She's in the Raigmore Hospital in Inverness. Had a stroke."

"When?"

"Last night. She was lucky. There was a local passing just as she keeled over in her living room. The curtains were drawn back and he saw her from the road and he had a mobile phone in his car, too. She could have lain there for days."

"So we come back again to Maggie Bane," said Hamish. "That's the trouble with this latest murder and this Kylie business. We're forgetting that Maggie Bane was the one with the real reason for hating Gilchrist. What if she knew or overheard his plans to go off with the terrible Mrs. Macbean? Then why did she go off for an hour that morning of all mornings? Damn, I think I'll go back and have a wee word with her."

"Better you than me," said Jimmy. "What an ugly voice that lassie has!"

Hamish found Maggie Bane in the middle of packing up her belongings. "What's happening?" he asked. "Are you leaving?"

"I can't stay here after all the scandal," she said in her harsh voice, that voice which sounded so odd coming out from such a beautiful face. "I'm going home to my parents. I'm putting this place up for sale."

"Do police headquarters know you are leaving?"

"Yes, I told them and left them my new address."

"You've heard about this latest murder?"

"Yes, I heard it on the radio this morning."

"And what do you make of it?"

She sat down on the floor beside a packing case as if suddenly weary. "It can't have anything to do with Mr. Gilchrist's murder."

"Well, Mr. Sutherland lived above the surgery and he left a message for me that he had found out something about Kylie Fraser."

Her face hardened. "That little slut!"

"Did you know Mr. Gilchrist tried to lay her?"

"That's her story. He told me she came on to him and got bitchy when he turned her down."

"Nothing about promising her a car if she kept her mouth shut?"

"Rubbish." Maggie's eyes blazed. "Let me tell you something, and I've already told the police this, Kylie Fraser is the biggest liar in the Highlands. She thought she could get any man she wanted and in order to fuel this myth, she made up wild stories." She stood up and began to lift books into one of the packing cases. Her arms, Hamish noticed, were very strong.

"If you don't mind my saying, Miss Bane," said Hamish, "you look verra fit. Take much exercise?"

"I play a lot of squash."

"Squash?"

"Yes, it's the only thing I'll miss about Braikie. There's a very good squash club. Didn't you know? Three nights a week. Mr. Dempster, who's got the biggest house in the town—he owns a factory in Inverness—had a squash court built onto his house and started the club."

"When exactly are you leaving?" asked Hamish.

"A week's time."

Hamish stood up. "I'll be in touch."

"I hope not," she said acidly. "I never want to see another policeman again."

Hamish hesitated in the doorway. "What will you do?"

"I got a letter from one of my old tutors this morning. The only person to write me a nice letter, I may add. He suggested I come and see him with a view to finding me a good job. He said a good way to get over a horrible experience like this was to be successful."

At least I've done some good, thought Hamish, by going to

see that tutor. Let's just hope that the only person I've been able to help doesn't turn out to be a murderess.

He went back into Braikie. As he walked up the stairs towards Fred Sutherland's flat, he met a forensic team coming down the stairs in their white overalls.

"Anything?" he asked hopefully.

The leading man shook his head. "Not a print anywhere apart from the old man's."

Hamish was turning away when he noticed a dark stain in the passageway leading to the stairs. "What's that?" he asked sharply. "Blood?"

The man grinned. "Dream on. We know what that is."

"And what's that?"

"Dog piss, Sherlock."

"Oh." Hamish stood irresolute. The forensic team looked at him impatiently. He pulled himself together and stood aside to let them past.

He wandered out in the street, pulled off his cap and scratched his fiery hair furiously. There was something there on the edge of his mind. A small boy chasing a ball cannoned into him, regained his balance and shouted, "Whit are ye standing there like a big drip o' nothing fur?" and then ran on. Now if I gave that horrible little boy a clip round the ear, thought Hamish, I would make headlines in the newspapers next day, be suspended from my job pending a full enquiry. Maybe that was what was up with Kylie and her friends. They had grown up in a world of lax teaching, lax morals, junk food for the body and junk food for the mind. Then there was this wretched business of believing children innocent and precious things. Hamish remembered his own childhood, running with his friends, barbarians all, but kept in check by the disciplines of police, church and school. So today murders by children were becoming distressingly common. Perhaps the bad old

days when all children were guilty until proved innocent in the
eyes of the adult world had something going for it. He found
he was getting cold and brought himself out of his musings.

He suddenly thought of Sarah and had a sharp desire to see
her again. There was nothing more he could be expected to do
that day and a pleasant evening and—hope upon hope—pleasant night with Sarah was just what he needed.

He arrived at Tommel Castle Hotel and went into reception.
"Hullo, Hamish," said Mr. Johnson. "Bad business, this murder
of the old man."

"Yes, I've just come from Braikie. Miss Hudson in?"

"Didn't you know? She's left."

"Gone?"

"Aye, she went up to see auld Angus and then she comes
back, all pinched and strained and asks for her bill. She phoned
from reception. I listened, of course."

"Of course," echoed Hamish in a hollow voice.

"She said, 'It's me, Sarah. Oh, darling, I've missed you so
much. I'm sorry I ran away. It's all been a terrible mistake. I'll
try to get the evening flight from Inverness. Can you meet me
at Heathrow?' Whatever he said, I don't know because I could
only hear her side of the conversation. Then she said, 'You will?
Oh, thank you, darling. I'll phone you from Inverness and con-
firm I'm on the plane. Love you, too.'"

"Wass it her husband?"

"I got an idea it was."

"Funny Priscilla didn't mention she was married. And," said
Hamish, growing angry, "it's even funnier that she didn't say a
blind word to me."

"Well, that's women for you."

Hamish slouched off. He felt truly miserable and rejected.
Perhaps she had left a note for him at the police station. But

when he got there, there was only an electricity bill lying on the doormat.

He sat down at his desk in the police office and buried his face in his hands. He shouldn't feel this bad. It had only been one night and she had backed away from him ever since.

He suddenly knew he could not sit in the police station on his own. He locked up and headed back to Braikie. He would investigate something, anything—anything to keep his mind off Sarah. Where to start, he wondered as the orange sodium lights of the town stained the nighttime Highland sky.

What about that squash club? Might pick up something about Maggie Bane that he did not already know.

He told the owner, Mr. Dempster, that he just wanted to watch the matches and was taken up to a long gallery above the squash courts. Maggie Bane was in one, smashing balls with great energy, her black hair flying. She was playing with a thin, grey-haired muscular woman. In the next court a small round man was playing a tall well-built fellow. Hamish was about to turn away, when he suddenly turned back and focused on the small round man. It was the pharmacist, Mr. Charles Cody. Hamish watched in amazement the speed and power the little man put into his game.

He went slowly down the stairs and let himself outside. A cold wind had sprung up, coming in from the west, bringing with it the smell of the sea.

Now here, thought Hamish, with a fast beating heart, was a man who would know how to make nicotine poison, a man with enough strength to heave the body of a dead dentist up into the chair.

But why? What reason?

Fred Sutherland had found out something about Kylie. Hamish, like everyone else, had assumed the something was about Kylie and Gilchrist. But just suppose that something had been about Kylie and her boss.

What sort of man was Cody really? He had strength. He certainly played a ruthless game of squash.

Wait a bit. His wife had said he had been out walking the dog.

But now he thought of it, that had been a very frightened dog.

There had been dog urine on the stairs leading up past the surgery to Fred's flat. Could forensic tell one dog's urine from another? Bound to.

But why? Why murder Gilchrist and then Fred?

Surely it might mean that Cody had been having an affair with Kylie. The dentist had been revenge and poor Fred because somehow the old man had let slip that he was going to tell what he knew.

He could go back into the club and question him. But he suddenly wanted the right scenario, the right setting to make the man crack.

And then he thought of the formidable Mrs. Cody. He would go to Cody's home and wait for his return.

CHAPTER TEN

Life is the art of drawing sufficient conclusions from insufficient premises.

—Samuel Butler

As he stopped outside the Codys' house, he hesitated before climbing down from the Land Rover. He should really contact Strathbane and tell them about his suspicions, about the dog urine. But would they listen? It was all so slight. And then would forensic be able to get anything from that urine? It would have dried by now. Better go ahead with it and see what he could find.

He rang the doorbell. Again Mrs. Cody opened the door. Her heavy face was truculent when she saw him. "What is it, officer? We have already made a statement to detectives today."

"I just wanted a wee word with Mr. Cody."

"He's not here."

"When will he be back?"

She sighed and squinted at her watch. "Any minute now. He's playing squash."

"May I please come in and wait for him?" Hamish smiled at her winningly.

"No," she said and slammed the door in his face.

Aye, I've got bags o' charm when it comes to dealing with the ladies, thought Hamish sourly.

He got back into the Land Rover and waited.

The door opened and Mrs. Cody approached. Hamish rolled down the window. "That police vehicle is lowering the tone of the place," she snapped.

"Well, we can't have that, can we?" said Hamish amiably. "I could just drive it round the corner and come back and wait indoors for Mr. Cody."

She gave him a baffled look and said, "Oh, very well."

Hamish parked his vehicle carefully out of sight of the house, not so much as to please Mrs. Cody as not to forewarn Mr. Cody that he was waiting for him.

He went back and she ushered him into what she called the "lounge." Mrs. Cody was watching a game show on television. She paid no further attention to Hamish. Suky, the little dog, trotted up to Hamish and jumped on his lap. He patted the dog's rough coat.

At last he heard a car approaching. The dog gave a sharp bark and jumped down from Hamish's lap and ran to the front door.

"I'm home," called Mr. Cody. Mrs. Cody did not reply. Someone was about to win a car or a packet of safety pins, depending on luck.

Hamish stood up as Mr. Cody walked into the room. "What's this?" he demanded angrily.

"I wondered if I might have a word with you in private," said Hamish.

"There is nothing that cannot be said in front of my wife."

"Very well," said Hamish, watching him closely. "On the

night Fred Sutherland was murdered, you said you were walking the dog. Now there was a stain of dog urine on the stairs leading up to Fred Sutherland's flat. Forensic will be able to identify the dog from the urine."

"Are you implying I murdered that old man?" he demanded.

"She's won the safety pins," commented Mrs. Cody. "She chose the wrong box. I knew it."

"If you want to play it the hard way," said Hamish, "we'll wait for the results."

"Then do that," he said coldly, "and take yourself out of my house before I call my lawyer."

Hamish began to waver in his conviction. There seemed to be nothing about the guilty man in the cold eyes facing him.

"Then we'll check," he said, "and I'll be back."

He went out to the Land Rover and was about to radio Strathbane when a sudden awful thought struck him. Instead, he drove fast back to Braikie and went into the stairway leading up to Fred Sutherland's flat. The lightbulbs had been replaced. He stared down where the stain of dog urine had been. It was scrubbed white, a cleaner patch on the grey of the stone. No wonder Cody had looked as if he had nothing to fear.

Hamish cursed under his breath. Now he had a rock-hard cold conviction that somehow Cody was the murderer. Why had he not thought of it before? A pharmacist was the obvious suspect. He should not have listened to all those voices telling him that anyone could make nicotine poison.

He drove back to the police station and phoned Jimmy Anderson. "Aye, Kylie's back at her home," said Jimmy. "What's it about?"

"Are you on duty tonight?"

"For another two hours. Why?"

"Hang on there, Jimmy, and wait for my call. I may have a murderer for you."

"What?"

"Trust me." Hamish rang off.

He went through to his living room and rummaged in a box under the table until he found a small tape recorder. He checked that it worked, put it in his pocket with the small microphone poking out.

Then he drove back to Braikie, to Kylie's flat.

He was buzzed into the hall. Kylie opened the door. "Not you again," she groaned.

"Yes, me," said Hamish. "It's truth time, Kylie. Let's go inside."

They sat down facing each other in Kylie's messy living room. Clothes lay scattered everywhere, empty Coke cans and bottles, and a plate with the remains of supper.

Kylie's face was scrubbed free of makeup, making her look very young. She was wearing a long T-shirt and nothing else as far as Hamish could see and her feet were bare.

"So shoot, copper," said Kylie, affecting a nasal American voice.

Hamish surreptitiously switched on the tape recorder.

"I know who did the murders," said Hamish.

"Who?"

"Your boss, Charles Cody."

Her face went quite blank and then she gave a shrill laugh. "That's havers. What proof d'ye have?"

"Would you believe it, Kylie, a bit o' dog piss."

She stared at him mulishly and waited.

"Aye, on the evening Fred Sutherland was murdered, your boss said he was innocently taking his wee dog for a walk. But there was dog urine in the passage leading to the stairs at Fred Sutherland's address and that dog urine came from Cody's dog. I've a soft spot for you, Kylie, and I thought I had better let you know that the game's up. I'm on my way to arrest him."

Her eyes were dilated with fright. "It had nothing to do with me."

"It had everything to do with you. He was having an affair with you, wasn't he?"

"Yes," she muttered.

"Louder," commanded Hamish.

"Yes, yes, yes!"

"So you are an accessory to murder."

"No," Kylie screamed. "No! I told him about Gilchrist and the way he treated me, that was all. I'm no' saying anything else!"

"You'll be on television and all the newspapers," said Hamish. "They'll all want to talk to this lassie who drives men to murder."

She sat staring at him, her mouth a little open. Then she shrugged. "It's no' my fault if the fellows go mad for me." Hamish began to relax. Kylie's enormous vanity was taking over.

"I'll tell you," she said, "but there's just you and me here, so I'll deny any knowledge of it."

"True. Go on."

"Well, Charlie—Mr. Cody—was always trying to feel me up in the shop. I mean, look at him. He's old." Fifty-something to Kylie was really old. "Then one day he says, 'If you're nice to me, Kylie, I'll leave you this business in my will. And I'll give you a wee bonus at the end of each month.'

"It's a good business and I know the work as well as him. Not the pharmacy stuff but if I had the business then I could employ a pharmacist mysel', some nice young man, not an old perv like him."

"But he was a fit man. He could have lived for years."

"I'm telling you, he's old," persisted Kylie with all the arrogance of youth. "The things he made me do, handcuffs, leather, all that. I made a mistake. I thought Gilchrist might be a better deal and I told him about Cody. Then when Gilchrist turned out to be a rat, I went and told Charlie. Charlie asked me if I had told Gilchrist about him and I said, yes, I had, and Gilchrist was a beast and I hadn't wanted to go wi' him but he had forced me. I mean, I'd come to rely on Charlie's bonuses and I didn't want them to stop. When I heard about the murder, I couldnae believe it. I wanted free o' Charlie, but he said he had done it for me, and I was fair frightened of him."

"You could have got rid of him by telling the police what you knew," Hamish pointed out.

"He said if I ever told anyone, he'd kill me," said Kylie. "But you know how it is, you have to tell someone, so I told Tootsie, not about the murder but how I was having an affair with Charlie and what a perv he was. She said we should get some of the boys in the pub to sort him out, but I panicked and said nobody must know. But the silly bitch told her grandfather, old Joe Gibbon. Joe Gibbon goes to the Old Timers and he must have told Fred Sutherland, because Fred dropped a note through my door. He said he'd found out about my affair with Charlie Cody and that he was going to tell the police. The old fool said he was a private investigator and if I came to see him first, he would take me to the police and make things easy for me."

"So you told Mr. Cody."

She nodded. "He said, 'Don't worry. I'll see to it.'"

"Look here, lassie," said Hamish wrathfully, "you're as bad as Lady Macbeth. Did it no' dawn on you that you were inciting the man to murder?"

Her face hardened. "I wanted that business. That business should have been mine. You know what my mother does? She's a brass nail."

"She may be a prostitute," said Hamish heavily, "but she does it for money. She doesnae get men to murder for her."

"Did I tell that old fool, Cody, to murder for me?" screeched Kylie.

"Look, what I don't understand," said Hamish, "is how you managed to keep it quiet in a place like this."

"Two of the flats here are empty and there's two elderly people in the others who go to bed early. You cannae really see who's going up to the house because of all the bushes and trees. He'd slip something in his wife's cocoa to make her sleep and then he'd join me, but most it was in the back of the shop after hours. If I hadnae told Tootsie, he wouldn't have gone for old Fred."

Hamish stood up. "We'll be back for you, Kylie."

"Aye, well, I'll deny everything I've said to you."

Hamish went out into the cold evening and took several gulps of fresh air. He drove to the nearest phone box instead of using the radio and talked rapidly to Jimmy Anderson, finishing with, "I'll wait for you outside Cody's."

Hamish waited patiently until he saw the cars arriving, Jimmy with his sidekick, Harry MacNab, in the first car, and four policemen in the second. Hamish, who had parked round the corner from the house, got down and said, "No Blair?"

Jimmy grinned. "Shame to disturb his beauty sleep. Do we drag the bugger straight to Strathbane?"

"No, he'll get in that lawyer I'm sure he got for Kylie and we'll have hard going. We take this tape in and play it to him."

"Right, it's your show, Hamish. Lead the way."

They all crowded on the doorstep while Hamish rang the bell. Cody had obviously not drugged his wife's cocoa that night, for after a few moments, she opened the door, wearing a dressing gown over her nightgown. "What is all this?" she demanded furiously.

"Get your husband—now," ordered Hamish. She stared at

him, and then at the detectives and police behind him. She turned away and went upstairs. They all crowded into the hall.

Charles Cody came down in his pyjamas. "I've had enough of this," he said. "What on earth do you want with me now?"

"Let's chust go into the living room," said Hamish. "There's something we want you to listen to."

He led the way. The two detectives and Hamish followed. The policemen waited in the hall.

Hamish solemnly cautioned the pharmacist and charged him with the murders of Gilchrist and Sutherland. A sheen of sweat covered the pharmacist's face. Mrs. Cody could be heard out in the hall demanding to know why she could not join her husband.

Hamish placed the tape recorder on the table. Cody buried his face in his hands as the tape began to turn and Kylie's voice sounded out loud and clear.

When it finished, he said in a dull voice, "You tricked her, Macbeth, you bastard. There was no proof. I remembered the dog taking a leak at the foot of the stairs and went and scrubbed it clean, just in case. You bastard. She called me a perv! I thought she loved me." His voice broke. He wailed, "She loved me! She said she loved me!" Then he began to sob.

They led him out to the car. Lights were on in all the neighbouring houses, people stood out on their steps, staring at the police, at the small figure of Cody being taken to the cars. Mrs. Cody joined her husband. As she got in the car, she said, "If by any chance you get off, Charles, I'll kill you myself. We were always so respectable."

"Weren't we just," he said savagely. "You with your ugly body and your respectable knickers. You make me sick."

"Are they bringing in Kylie?" asked Hamish when they reached Strathbane.

Jimmy nodded. "And she's in for a shock when she hears that tape. We'll need to wait for that lawyer. Cody insists on that. Want a cup of tea afore he arrives? They've gone to get him out of bed."

"Aye, that would be grand," said Hamish.

They went up to the canteen. "Good work, Hamish," said Jimmy. "You did well and no cowboy tactics. This'll mean promotion for you."

Hamish looked at him thoughtfully. "Unless you say the whole thing was your idea."

"What?"

"Think about it, Jimmy. A feather in your cap. Promotion would mean Strathbane for me."

"I don't want to do a Blair on you, Hamish, but I'd be right glad to take the credit. What do you want?"

Hamish grinned. "Peace and quiet."

"Well, here's to you," said Jimmy, raising his teacup.

Hamish suddenly stiffened. "They'd get Cody to turn out his pockets, wouldn't they?"

"Aye, that's the form. What are you thinking of, Hamish?"

"I'm thinking of poison. I hope they took any pills off him."

Jimmy stared at Hamish wide-eyed. "Unless the bugger said they were heart pills or something and being a pharmacist, whatever would be in the right bottle."

They both ran for the door.

"Of course we got him to turn out his pockets," said the desk sergeant contemptuously. Cody had been allowed to dress before they had taken him from his home. "He had nothing on him but a handkerchief and his house keys and car keys."

"No medicine?"

"He had his asthma pills."

"But you kept them?"

"No. It seemed all right to—"

"Which cell is he in?" shouted Jimmy.

"Number five. But—"

"Open it now!"

Looking sulky, the desk sergeant went and unlocked cell number five. Mr. Charles Cody lay as dead as a doornail on the floor.

"So it all ended up a right mess," said Hamish on the phone to Priscilla the following day. "Of course Blair arrived in the morning and tried to sabotage Jimmy's catch by saying if he'd have been called out, Cody would still have been alive."

"So what happens to Kylie?"

"She'll appear in court charged with accessory to murder and incitement to murder and impeding the police in their enquiries. But that expensive lawyer's probably going to defend her for free. He likes the publicity. He'll make mincemeat of me at the trial and Kylie will probably walk free and sell her story to the newspaper that pays the most and live a happy selfish life forever after." There was a little silence and then Hamish said with affected casualness, "I didn't know Sarah was married."

"Yes, she had a bust-up with her husband. Didn't I tell you? Oh, no, I remember, we didn't mention Sarah."

"She might have told me," said Hamish.

"Why should she?" demanded Priscilla sharply.

"Well, we had dinner a few times. I thought she might have mentioned it."

"If she was hurting," said Priscilla, her voice now heavy with suspicion, "she would hardly tell a village policeman she barely knew."

Hamish decided it was time to change the subject. "The only thing that puzzles me is that hour that Maggie Bane took the morning of the murder. I think I'll go and ask her before she leaves."

"I must say all this ferocious murder and passion in a place like Braikie comes as a surprise."

"I suppose any passion would come as a surprise to you, Priscilla."

"Goodbye, Hamish."

There was a click as she rang off. Hamish swore furiously. Why had he said that? It wasn't as if he cared for Priscilla anymore.

Did he?

Maggie Bane answered the door to him, looking relaxed and cheerful for the first time. "Come in," she said. "I was just about to have a cup of coffee. Join me?"

Hamish nodded.

"You'll need to sit on the floor. The furniture's gone off to storage."

Hamish sat down on the floor and looked around the empty room. After a few minutes, Maggie came in with a tray with two mugs of coffee on it. She placed it on the floor between them.

"The nightmare's over," she said.

"Did you suspect Cody?"

"No, and that's the funny thing. He called in to the surgery a week before the murder and Mr. Gilchrist put his head round the surgery door and ordered me to go for a walk. Said they had something private to discuss."

"Why didn't you tell me?" demanded Hamish.

"He was the pharmacist. He supplied our drugs. I didn't think anything of it."

"Clear up one other thing for me," said Hamish. "That hour

off you took on the day of the murder. Was there more to that than you told me?"

She looked at him for a long time in silence and then gave a little shrug. "The fact is we'd had a blazing row the night before. I went in at ten and gave him his coffee. He usually left it until it got nearly cold. I suppose that's what gave Cody the opportunity to put poison in it. I told him I was leaving him. I was putting on my coat and just walking out. He could find another receptionist. I went round the shops, did all those things I'd told you I did, and then I thought I may as well go back and pick up the few things I'd left in the surgery."

"Why didn't you tell me?"

"I thought if I did you'd suspect me of the murder. But surely Cody took a great risk. I could have just walked in. Anyone could have seen him going up the stairs to the surgery."

"We got it out of Kylie during the night when she finally broke. He had told her he was so mad with rage and passion, he didn't care if anyone found him. At first he just meant to poison Gilchrist and walk away. He'd been up at the surgery before and knew when Gilchrist had his coffee and how he left it to get nearly cold. He said when he was finally dead, his rage would not go away and that's why he hauled him into the chair and drilled his teeth. It was only afterwards when he realised how lucky he had been, that he began to relax. Besides Kylie said it gave him an extra hold over her. She was frightened if she told anyone, he would kill her. And with him dead, there's no one to contradict her story. Her lawyer will get her dressed up like an innocent schoolgirl for the trial and she'll sob and say he threatened her into silence and everyone will believe her. You obviously know Cody's dead."

"Yes, it was on the radio this morning."

"They've got a mole at headquarters. The papers aye get

something the moment it happens. Which reminds me. There's something I've got to do."

Hamish said goodbye to her and drove to the Old Timers Club where he found Tam.

"I'm going to give you the name o' a nice reporter on the *Inverness Daily,*" said Hamish. "Do you have a photo of Fred?"

"Aye," said Tam.

"Give it to the reporter with a story about Fred Sutherland, detective, about how he broke the case. I think Fred would have liked that."

"Oh, my," said Tam, "he would hae been in seventh heaven."

"I'll write out what I want you to say," said Hamish, "and bring it back to you."

Hamish then went back to the dress shop and confronted Mrs. Edwardson. "Do you know that it was Charles Cody who murdered Mr. Gilchrist and Fred Sutherland?"

"Yes, I heard it on the breakfast news. Who would have thought it? Such a pillar of the community and always a pleasant word for everyone. I mean, when I saw him that morning, I didn't think anything of it."

"What morning?" shouted Hamish.

"There's no need to take that tone of voice with me, officer." She flushed a mottled red. "If you must know, he passed the shop window on the morning of the murder and I think I heard him go up the stairs."

"You stupid auld bitch," roared Hamish. "Why didn't you tell me?"

"One doesn't think. I mean such a respectable man. I mean . . ."

"Fred Sutherland would have been alive if it hadn't been for you," said Hamish bleakly. He went out and slammed the door of the shop behind him.

And that, he thought, as he drove off, was what had contrived to make the case so baffling—a mixture of snobbery, amateurism and sheer luck. Cody must have thought the gods were on his side when he wasn't accused of the murder of Gilchrist. But what passion Kylie must have fired in that respectable middle-aged bosom!

Lochdubh began to prepare for Christmas. Fairy lights were strung from the cottages to the standard lamps on the waterfront. Christmas trees appeared in cottage windows, fake Christmas trees. There were fir trees all over the surrounding hills but the housewives of Lochdubh did not want the business of vacuuming pine needles from their carpets and so there were plastic trees of silver and gold and of an improbable green.

Archie Macleod had a bright green plastic tree in his garden and was decorating it with Christmas lights as Hamish stopped for a chat.

"Not allowed to have the thing indoors, Archie?" said Hamish sympathetically.

"No, herself would neffer allow a Christmas tree but I am having this one this year. A man must take a stand sometime, Hamish."

Hamish grinned and moved on. He quickened his pace as he passed the Currie sisters' cottage, not wanting to be waylaid. The Currie sisters alone did not have any Christmas decorations, following the old Scottish Calvinistic belief that Christmas decorations were sinful.

He then went into Patel's store to see if there was anything he could pick up for Christmas presents for his family in Rogart to save him a journey to Strathbane. The shop smelled of Christmas pudding and spices. He could not see anything suitable and resigned himself to the thought of a trip to Strathbane.

When he walked back to the police station, he found Jimmy Anderson waiting for him.

"I've brought the stuff this time," said Jimmy, clutching two carrier bags. Hamish let him into the kitchen. Jimmy put a large turkey on the table and two bottles of whisky. "Least I could do, Hamish," he said. "Blair tried to spoil things for me over Cody's suicide but the super pointed out I'd done a smart bit of work and couldn't be blamed for something the desk sergeant was guilty of. Mind you, the super's pretty sure it was your doing but I've got a good success on my record and I'll hae Blair's job out from under his fat arse or my name isn't Jimmy Anderson. I tell you, Blair's on the wagon these days and he's like a bear with a sore bum."

"Has he joined AA?"

"Do you mean the Automobile Association or Alcoholics Anonymous?"

"Alcoholics Anonymous."

"Naw, his doctor recommended it but Blair said he wasnae going to be seen dead with a lot of God botherers."

"Lucky for you," said Hamish.

"Why?"

"Och, it is just that the folks who go to AA in Strathbane seem to put down the drink and take up success like ducks to water."

"Jings, you're right. Archie Pattock, the town drunk, him what used to be in rags and vomit, used to go about saying he was an electronics engineer, well the AA's got hold o' him and now he's working for one o' those big places over in Tayside and it turns out he was an electronics engineer right enough. Got a big car. Oh, my, I just pray Blair never gets to one o' their damn meetings. And talking of AA, what about us opening one o' these bottles?"

After Jimmy had left, Hamish went out again. A blazing sunset was going down over the hills and mountains. The loch was pink and gold. The fairy lights twinkled on along the length of the waterfront.

He stood breathing in the evening air scented with pine and felt at peace with the world.

And then as he looked along the waterfront, he saw Priscilla standing there, looking out at the loch. She was wearing a Christmas-red woolen coat and a tartan scarf. The lights shone on the golden bell of her hair.

Then she turned as if aware of his presence.

For one long moment, Hamish Macbeth and Priscilla Halburton-Smythe stared at each other down the length of the waterfront. From the church, children's voices were singing "Come All Ye Faithful."

Then Priscilla turned on her heel and walked away, got into her car and drove off.

Hamish Macbeth was not to be forgiven.